West of the Moon

Jonathan Nasaw

WEST *of the* MOON

Franklin Watts   New York Toronto

For Judith

West of the Moon

Chapter

1

Danny Dawson was five years old when they let him out of the hospital early in June. He was bald, his scalp stencilled with blue lines, and his skin sallow and shiny as cheese, all of which made it hard for his mother to flag down a cab. A Yellow passed them by, then a Luxor, then another Yellow. Anne looked down at the boy in the obligatory hospital-discharge wheelchair. "If the next one doesn't stop, I'll give him the Ernestine face," she said, narrowing her eyes and setting her jaw like Lily Tomlin's doughty operator.

Danny laughed. "Yeah!" The Ernestine face was his mom's way of telling him she would not, for instance, let the nurses separate the two of them for this test or that, would not let the lab tech stick *just one more* needle in his arm, *would* bring his best stuffed penguin to him in Post-Op even if the Wicked Witch of the West were standing guard.

But the next driver did stop. He looked like Howdy Doody with a goatee, wore a rainbow-striped knit watch cap, and helped Danny into the cab with a simple kindness that sent gratitude welling up in Anne's chest. She gave him the address for the Casa de Vida. "That a hospital?" He threw the meter and eased out into traffic.

"It's a halfway house. I haven't seen it yet."

"Well, I can tell you it's in a nice neighborhood, anyway. Lots of times I pick up people at the hospital that look like the boy there, and I have to take'm to some hole in the Tenderloin. You folks are lucky."

"I suppose," said Anne. "Of course, there's lucky and then there's lucky."

A few minutes later Danny opened his eyes to find himself in a typical San Francisco neighborhood of wooden houses and sun white sidewalks. The bottle-brush trees were in bright red bloom, and their shadows, blue-edged black, shimmered in the glare. "I guess this is it," said the driver, pulling up to a handsome white Victorian with blue trim and a complicated Charles Addams roofline of turrets, gables, skylights, and dormer windows. "There's no sign or anything, though."

Anne was dubious. "I'll be right back, hon," she said, and patted Danny, who had shut his eyes against a surge of nausea. She trotted up the high white wooden steps and knocked at the painted door, waited, knocked again.

"Hold your horses," someone called. She heard heavy uneven footsteps, and the door was opened by a frightfully tall man leaning on a knotty cane of Irish blackthorn. "Ah," he said. "I thought you were the drugstore."

"I'm not."

"No, you don't look like a drugstore." Not even a little. She had a pleasant round face with spots of high color on either cheek and eyes the color of light brown m&m's; her hair was a dark unreflective brown.

"*Thank* you. Is this the Casa de Vida?"

"Yes ma'am. Roomers with Tumors."

"I'm Anne Dawson."

He smiled. "I'm Tom Straw. Been expecting you." He switched the cane to his left hand and bent down carefully to shake her hand. Tom's face was long and plain; he had lank blond hair for which there was no fashionable cut—spent twenty dollars in a "salon" once and still came out looking like Will Rogers. "We've got a room all ready for you and Danny. Dr. Hoffman's in Omaha for another week or so—I'm the rest of the staff." He followed Anne back down the steps, his heart quickening the way it always did when a new patient came to the Casa. Just a little stage fright—he fell back on his bedside manner. "Beautiful day to be out of the hospital, hey, Danny?" He opened the door to the back of the cab.

"If I try to walk I'll throw up," the boy said quietly.

"I'll bet the driver here would rather have you throw up on the sidewalk than the back seat."

"If it's all the same to you," said the cabbie.

Danny's face, puffy from the medication, and his plump cheeks and browless eyes gave him a deceptively placid look, but his glance was quick and uncertain as he climbed stiffly out of the cab, holding onto the door for balance.

"You gonna make it?" asked Tom. The boy rolled his eyes.

"Don't worry about the sidewalk. We had one guy, named Chuck, used to throw up on it every time he came back from the hospital. Used to call him Upchuck. You want to try the steps or take the elevator up from the basement?"

Danny looked from Tom to the steps and back. "I can make it," he said. "What happened to your leg?"

Anne winced and turned back to pay the driver.

"First they cut it off to right about"—Tom measured, palm down at his side—"about your height, then they burned it."

Danny nodded matter-of-factly. "Did you have cancer?"

"Yup."

Danny started up the steps; Tom lurched behind him, one hand on the rail for balance, one hand free, cane under his arm, to spot the boy.

"Did you get radiationed and chemicalled?"

"Yup."

"You got hair."

"It grew back. It almost always grows back."

Danny started to wobble just below the landing. Tom steadied the boy with a hand the size of a frying pan against the small of his back. "I got you," he said.

"You got me, who's got you?" Danny replied. It was a joke he remembered from *Superman*.

Tom laughed. "Louie," he said, quoting from another movie, "I think this is the beginning of a beautiful friendship."

"Who's Louie?"

"Claude Rains."

"Oh."

———

The carpets, the dark wooden balustrade of the front staircase, the patterned waist-high wainscoting, and heavy panelled doors gave the house a certain creepy Victorian dignity that Danny liked. The Casa seemed mysterious to him, with its high dramatic ceilings, round archways, oddly angled corners, niches, bay windows, and the promise of secret places to explore. It was different as could be from the right angles and cool hospital pastels he had known for months.

He changed into his *Star Wars* pajamas while Tom helped

Anne hang his penguin posters and Giants pennants in the front second-floor bedroom. He was too tired to explore the house, but afraid to nap alone, afraid his brain would swell up: he'd overheard a resident on rounds say something about that side effect of the radiation. He told Anne. *I don't know how to comfort him with words anymore,* she thought, and sat with him, held his hand and stroked his scalp until he fell asleep. She noticed that the crook of his arm was bruised the color of a Tequila Sunrise. *Lamb,* she thought. *Mommy can't kiss and make it better anymore.* She thought of him as he'd been at three—sturdy little bulldog with a rolling tough guy walk and the buns you love to bite—but forced herself to stop before the tears could take hold. *It's too early to start remembering him,* she scolded herself. *That's just giving up.*

Chapter

2

Danny awoke late in the afternoon, alone in his room, disoriented but no longer nauseous. He tried to think whether this was a Pill day or a Shot day. Then he remembered that it was neither, and that he was in the hospital that was really a house, where there was a man named Straw who had hair like straw. Next he tried to remember whether he was supposed to pee in the *carafe*, as his mother called it, or whether he could go to the toilet by himself—the rules kept changing. The shiny bars of his hospital bed were up so he climbed carefully over the footboard, found the bathroom, peed, took his yellow terry cloth bathrobe from the oval brass doorknob, and wandered off to find his mom, his fingers trailing reassuringly along the bumpy wainscoting. He didn't like the looks of the elevator cage, and took the stairs, his feet in soft tan slippers padding down the carpeted steps, left hand caressing the dark smooth wood of the bannister.

The front parlor had the still, dusted look of a room where kids weren't allowed. Danny peeked in from the arched doorway. A low marble coffee table and an apple green sofa rested on a fat, elegantly patterned carpet. There was a brick fireplace with brass andirons; a great antique samovar gleamed dully on the mantelpiece. Danny's fingers itched to turn all the intricate little faucets and flip back the tiny hinged spout lids, but he heard his mother calling him from the kitchen at the end of the hallway, and shuffled on back.

The kitchen was a high-ceilinged orange and white room with wide counters and an oak table that expanded like one of the Chinese Brothers in the storybook to accommodate everyone who showed up for meals. Anne was starting to come alive again after the hospital months, turning over slowly like an old car on a cold morning. She'd shared a bottle of Rainier Ale, known as Green Death, with Linda Sanchez, one of the patients, before they'd started cooking, and she was just a tad bubbly. She stood at the stove turning the squash in the lemon butter: *how pretty it was: pale spring green and yellow.* The radio played some recent Stones *(better than no Stones at all,* she thought), and she found herself moving to the music—a slide and a glide and a dip with the hip—as Danny padded in.

"Hi, sweetie. Did you have a nice nap?"

"I guess. I don't know. I was asleep." He climbed onto one of the ladder-back kitchen chairs and watched Linda, a short, sleepy-eyed woman with a wide-bridged nose and a crew-length growth of fuzzy hair, snapping the leaves off a head of dark red lettuce and tossing them into the plastic bin of the salad washer. She washed the lettuce and watercress at the sink, still moving somewhat stiffly after her mastectomy, then brought the bin back to the table for Danny to turn the crank while she sliced tomatoes.

"These tomatoes are so ripe you need a razor to cut them before they squish," Linda said over her shoulder to Anne.

"They're better than those Mexican tomatoes Safeway had all winter." Anne lowered the flame on the burner.

"I remember. You could play tennis with those." Linda noticed Danny staring at her hair. "Here, would you like to feel somethin' nice?"

She bent her head over the table and he stroked the softness of the new hair: it ruffed back like fur and tickled his palm. "Did you have cancer and your hair fell out but it grew back?" he asked.

"That's right." The boy's small hand felt intensely sensual—Linda purred and arched her neck back against the pressure like a cat. Sometimes she felt so terribly glad to be alive that her senses were filled by strange bright things: the red of the tomatoes, the little boy's insistent touch.

Danny watched his mother cook awhile, then tugged at the belt loop of her jeans. "Can I go watch tv?"

"We don't have a tv."

"I hear one on in that room there."

He pointed toward the back bedroom, a big lozenge-shaped room that had been converted from a dining room for the occasional terminal patient who preferred to stay at the Casa rather than transfer to a hospice. It was an excellent room in which to die: light, airy, just off the kitchen around which the social life of the house revolved, but soundproofed for privacy. The current occupants were Toni Conroy and Bea Levitt. Toni was the patient, her cancer in a state of galloping metastasis. She was by now too weak to leave her bed, so she'd had them set her up so she could look out through the bay window, beyond the garden below to the sheltered valley of backyards, flower beds, toolsheds, shade trees, balconies, service porches, clotheslines and rock gardens that sloped steeply from Diamond Heights. Bea was a keen woman with wiry red hair and pale-lidded eyes. She spent most of her days in a rocking chair in the bend of the bay window, knitting Toni an afghan against the cold summer ahead, and slept at night on a futon on the floor.

Danny walked in lopsidedly but confidently, having grown used to strangers in the past months. The fawn-colored walls had a rosy tinge from the light of the western sun, and the room was stuffed with flowers in vases, jars, cups and glasses, yet a stale sour smell lingered. Danny knew it from the hospital. His glance took in the urine bag clipped to the lower bed rail and the boxes of adult diapers and Chux in the corner, skipped past the sleeping woman on the bed and fixed on the red-haired woman in the rocker. "What're you watching?"

"The usual crap," Bea whispered. She hadn't been paying attention—she just liked the electronic murmur. "Come on in." She moved her knitting bag over to make room for him on the window seat. He climbed up and glanced at the screen—*news: yuck*—and looked out over the garden. The magnolia and the roses were in fat pink bloom, and the jasmine climbing the trellis was white as soap.

"Look, that cat's dreaming." He pointed to a black cat lying on its side under the forsythia, forepaws twitching in its sleep. There were several cats who slept in different homes, but considered the backyard valley their commons.

"I see. But let's whisper—I think Toni's sleeping."

"Does she have cancer?"

"No, she's not sleeping and yes, she does have cancer," said Toni, opening her light blue eyes, big as grapes in her fine-boned face.

"Did *your* hair fall out but it grew back in?"

Toni nodded. Her second-growth was in thin blond curls.

"That's good to know," said Danny solemnly.

"I know, it's not any fun to be bald," said Toni. *"I* had a wig at first. I also had a . . . *wait* just a minute: Bea, is my Giants cap still around?"

"I'll get it." Bea put aside her knitting and stood up. Danny held his breath. It *sounded* like they were going to give him a present, but he was afraid to ask. Maybe they only wanted to show him. But sure enough when Bea returned with a black, orange-billed, one-size-fits-all Cap Day Giants cap, she placed it carefully on his head and helped him adjust the plastic strap in back. "Perfect fit," she said. "Doesn't he look sharp?"

"That's a present now," said Toni. "You can keep that."

"But when my hair grows back I might give it to some other kid with cancer who's bald, right?"

"That would be very nice."

"I know." He pulled the cap around backwards like a catcher; the bill drooped over the back of his neck. "For good luck," he explained, and trooped back to the kitchen to show his mom.

———

Danny looked down at his plate disconsolately. He'd never much liked salad, and the color of the squash, which had so delighted his mother, looked to him like caterpillar guts. "Tom Straw?"

"Yes, Danny Dawson?"

"In this house do I have to eat all my dinner to get dessert?" Tom had offered to take them out for ice cream.

"Your mom's the boss."

"Mom?"

"Honey, you *should* eat *something.*"

"What's your favorite food for dinner?" Tom asked.

"SpaghettiOs."

Tom looked at Anne, who nodded. "Feel like a trip to the store?" he asked the boy.

"How far?"

"Ten miles."

"Aw, come on."

"Just up at the corner." Tom faced the front of the house and pointed right. "The guy's name's Abdul, but everybody calls him Mr. Abe. Take the food stamp book out of the coffee can over there. Tell him you're from the Casa de Vida, he'll give you change. Smile at his wife, she'll give you some awful Arab candy."

"I *like* awful Arab candy," said Danny and marched off, listing to the right, clutching the food stamp book to his breast with his good left hand. "See you later, alligator."

Anne returned the password. "After awhile, crocodile."

The store was dark and cluttered and smelled wonderfully of old biscuits, sour milk, and dusty paper cartons. Mr. Abe had wet brown eyes; the chinless Mrs. Abe did indeed come through with some translucent orange brown candy that crumbled dryly in the boy's mouth. He felt very grown up to be carrying home the familiar red and white can, with the correct change jingling in his pocket.

Tom heated up the SpaghettiOs for Danny with a bachelor's dispatch, turning the burner up past welding heat and tossing the noodles frantically with a fork. Danny ate them dreamily, delighting in the mushy round surrender of the noodles and the metallic aftertaste of the thin red sauce.

After dinner Tom drove the Dawsons and Linda to a Double Rainbow ice-cream shop on 24th Street, where an illuminated rainbow was reflected into infinity by two great mirrors on opposing walls. Danny zombied out, staring into the illusion, watching himself, and his ever smaller selves, whittling away at the cone. He was so fascinated that when he went to bed that night he thought, as he fell asleep, not of his brain swelling, or the dead man in ICU, or of any of his terrible hospital dreams, but of RAINBOWRAINBOWrainbow shrinking to nothing but extending forever. He thought he would be very happy to live in the Casa de Vida with his mother and Tom Straw for a long long time.

3

Make me a pallet on your floor. Anne thought of the old song as she lay on her foam pad keeping Danny company while he fell asleep. She was not at all sleepy herself. The Casa de Vida was a garden of night-blooming sounds—a creak, a cough, the elevator clanking like Marley's ghost—but above all Anne was aware of Danny's breathing. He sounded . . . like a kid sleeping, only a kid sleeping. If she closed her eyes she could imagine they were back in the Baker Street apartment they'd had to give up, along with Anne's job as a legal secretary at the Public Defender's office, when Danny had fallen ill. *Six months ago. Not quite six months.* She shuddered in recollection. *Never mind that now. Don't think about that. Think about how far we've come.* She sat up, knelt on the mattress, and with her chin resting on the window ledge, parted the curtains just far enough to peek out at the empty street, the live oak, the haze of the streetlights, and the thick bushes across the street writhing in the wind. *At least we're out of the goddam hospital.* She rummaged in her suitcase—she had unpacked Danny's things but not her own— for her old mustard-colored Irish fisherman's sweater, pulled it over her head, kissed her sleeping boy, and tiptoed out, leaving the door carefully ajar.

The office of the Casa was squeezed into an unused corner of the attic. Tom Straw was going over Danny's hospital records, which were in two fat manilla folders, when he heard Anne climbing the stairs. He looked around the room distractedly, then limped into the storeroom— he was training himself not to use his cane—and dragged a folding chair back for her. "How's Danny?"

"Asleep. He was exhausted."

They were each in jeans; Tom wore a faded black pocket T-shirt under a green plaid Pendleton wool shirt so old and soft the buttons had just worn away. He saw her glance behind him to the manilla folders on the desk. "You're welcome to read any of this stuff you want to," he said. "In fact, it'd be a good idea."

"What's the point?" she said flatly. "I know how it comes out."

They stared at each other for a moment. Tom's eyes were mild and blue. "How *does* it come out?" he asked.

She felt the panic rising like a bubble under her heart and broke the eye contact, glancing around the windowless office as if it could prompt her. *You know,* she thought. *You know.* She saw papers and journals, desk clutter, a small refrigerator with an unlocked bicycle lock around it, a filing cabinet, bills speared on a spindle. An unframed sheet of notepaper was tacked to one of the rough-finished redwood beams that striped the slanted ceiling. "Turn out the light," she read. "The dawn is coming." At first it was senseless as one of the scrambled word puzzles in the Chronicle; then it struck her. Tears filled her eyes; she brushed them away.

"You can cry here," said Tom.

"I cried once," she said, and blinked hard. "They stuck me with a needle so fast I barely had time to get my pantyhose down."

"When was that?"

"After Danny's operation. The funny thing is, I *never* wear pantyhose. But for some reason I dressed up that morning as if I were being interviewed for a job."

"What'd they tell you?"

"That they'd taken out all they could reach. That it was malignant. I asked them if he were going to die, and they reeled off the percentages for me. *Percentages.* I wanted to grab that Dr. Bruner by the lapels and shake him. But instead I started crying, and the other doctor, the pediatrician . . ." She depressed an imaginary hypodermic plunger with her thumb, and shrugged.

Tom shook his head. "Frightening," he said. "Pavlov woulda been proud. I guess *they* taught *you.* I'll tell you something about Bruner, though: it's not that he doesn't care. Hell, he'll stay up all night chasing through the most obscure journals, scared to death somebody someplace made a breakthrough that could save his patient, and he won't know about it. But he could no more hold somebody's hand or sit at a bedside than, than quack like a duck. There's a lot of men and women go into medicine 'cause they *hate* death, *hate* suffering: they're just *petrified* with denial."

"That's nice to know," said Anne, who could still feel that bubble under her heart—"but where does it leave Danny?"

"Downstairs sleeping with six stuffed penguins. Where does it leave you?"

"All strangled up." Then Anne surprised herself immensely: she began to cry. The sense of release was nearly pleasurable, almost like when she was nursing Danny and the milk would first let down. Tom pushed himself up from his chair; kneeling awkwardly he reached his long arms around her. She wept with her face in her hands, then against his shoulder; he felt the shuddering clear through to his bones. When she had finished she sniffled and said into his shirt: "So what should I do now?" She'd intended it as a sort of pleasantry, but the words wobbled out.

He shrugged. "There's a mattress and a rubber hose down in the screaming room in the basement. If I was you I'd go down there and beat the shit out of the one with the other."

———

Anne didn't think it would work at first, and she felt silly alone on her knees in a square white room in the basement, flailing away at the striped mattress ticking with a two-foot length of black rubber hose. The sound was wrong, for one thing—a flat dull thwack—when what she longed for was the resonance of a watermelon hitting cement. She kept at it, though, and soon her mind took up a rhythm—you *fuck*er, you *fuck*er, you *fuck*er—and each time she raised her arm over her head she could feel a pulling of the muscles that stretched from shoulder to breast, of the cords that bound her lungs so tightly in her rib cage, a pulling and a loosening, and she began to breathe into every blow and her constricted grunts opened out to full sobs and *you fucker, you fucker* turned in her mind to *my* boy, not *my* boy. . . . She threw the hose away as if it were a snake and collapsed forward onto the mattress, crying "not my boy, not my boy, not my boy" until her heart eased, and she heard herself, and thought: *If not my boy, whose? Whose boy then?* And the angry, empty place inside her was filled with a simple sorrow that was very like compassion, and that helped her sleep that night, and for many nights thereafter.

4

It was still dark when Tom Straw hopped down the hall to and from the bathroom the next morning. He pulled on a stump sock and smoothed out the wrinkles, strapped on his leg and dressed to a thin gray light just bright enough to hide the stars, then took the back stairs up to the office so the clatter of the elevator wouldn't wake the house.

Before going to bed he had poured Toni's daily dose of Brompton's mix into a bowl of lime jello and brought it up to the office to set. In the morning the green gel shimmered in the pale attic light. Blessed Brompton's, Dr. Hoffman called it: morphine and cocaine stilled the pain but left the patient conscious. Tasted like road tar, though: Tom's friend Dr. Krebs, who ran a hospice up in Bigfoot County, had come up with the jello idea, which worked like a charm.

Tom limped down two flights of stairs. The door to the back bedroom was open; he ducked through the doorway bearing the bowl before him. Toni's back was to the door—the curtains were open and she was watching the morning fog drifting down across the valley of backyards—but she felt the old dining room floor under the green carpet rock with Tom's uneven step. "Hi, Big Nurse," she said.

Tom put the bowl down on her bedside table as Bea emerged from the bathroom. "It's the Pusher Man," said Bea cheerfully, toweling vigorously at her head; when she crossed in front of the window her carroty hair was a bright splotch of color against the sleepy gray mist.

Toni's hand shook as she scooped out the doped green jello; the stuff wobbled on the spoon as she brought it to her mouth.

"Rough night?" asked Tom.

"She had a good deal of pain," Bea answered for her, then took the empty spoon from Toni's hand. "Need another?" Toni shook her head. Bea wiped off the spoon with a paper towel and put it beside the bowl. "She finally took a Percodan around two."

"I don't like those dopey sleeps," Toni explained.

"Or the Happy, Grumpy and Bashful ones," said Tom. "Tell you what, I'll come by tonight with some tapes and color squares, we can do some relaxation and visualization work."

"That sounds fine," said Toni. She was mostly just glad the damn long night was over.

Tom and Bea worked together as the fog obscured the hillside. They changed Toni's bed, Chux and urine bag, diaper and nightgown, and redressed the dime-sized bedsore at the base of her spine. Then while Bea carried the stinking trash bag down to the garbage bin in the basement, Tom took Toni's temperature and checked her pulse, warmed his stethoscope with his breath, and reached under her cotton flannel nightgown modestly to listen to her heart and lungs. She was no prude, but he knew that after a year of being handled like meat in various hospitals she didn't like to be exposed unnecessarily.

"How do I sound?" she asked.

"Like a '56 Chevy with twenty thousand miles."

"Flatterer."

Bea had stopped by the garden on her way up to pick some more flowers. She washed out an empty mayonnaise jar and arranged a bouquet for Toni, placed it on the windowseat, then returned to the kitchen to blend Toni's breakfast smoothie. Tom had gone back to the office to prepare Danny's morning medication. Toni sighed and lay back, grateful for the day and the peaceful rush of the morphine and cocaine. She'd had them raise the head of her bed and prop her up so she could look down into the garden, where Linda had taken Danny for a romp so Anne could sleep late. She watched the boy hop about delightedly, clapping his hands with each new discovery: after spending the last tenth of his life indoors, every worm, snail and flower knocked him out, and even a *three*-leaf clover was a lucky strike.

————

Sunset that evening, as seen from Toni's bed, was a reflected glory, a diffuse pink glow above a fog bank high and gray as a battleship.

Dying was not meeting Toni's expectations. It wasn't any worse, you understand. She'd just thought these last few weeks or months (if not of life then of awareness: it was getting harder to keep the Brompton's down, and if the pain grew much worse she fantasized asking Tom just to knock her unconscious with the dope and the hell with life's last great adventure) would be different, every moment precious. Instead she grew daily more indifferent to the passage of time.

Her dreams, on the other hand, were intensely vivid now, but getting harder to remember when she was awake. And vice-versa: the "I" of her dreams, the dreamer, had only a vague sense of something important, barely forgotten.

She watched the sunset for a while, then fell asleep again to the comforting click and whisper of Bea's knitting needles and dreamed for the first time of her father, who'd passed away in January. In her dream it was already the Fourth of July: she could hear the firecrackers in the night. He spoke to her. Words of welcome. "Dad," she said. "Remember? . . ." Just before he died there'd been a terrible family fight about her wanting to bring Bea home with her for the holidays. Toni had ended up not going herself. "Oh that," he chuckled. "With the grace of God and a shovelful of Valium we managed to calm your mother down. But none of that matters anymore. Not for us."

She awoke, chilled and sure, but not frightened. Bea noticed . . . something. "What is it, baby?"

"I had a dream about my father."

"It was only a dream."

"No," said Toni. "No, it wasn't." It was like Dorothy waking up in Kansas and everybody telling her Oz was just a dream. "It wasn't exactly real, but it wasn't just a dream." And somehow she knew that a plateau of strength and lucidity and not too much pain had been reached, and that there was something she had to do. "Bea?"

"What?"

"Get Tom please?"

Bea hurried up to Tom's room. He limped back to the elevator with her; it clanked into reluctant life.

Toni felt the dining room floor rock, then saw Tom's face, big as a balloon, looming over her. "Bea," she whispered. "I need a few minutes alone with Tom. Don't worry. Everything is fine."

———

Don't think, don't think, don't think, thought Bea. She opened the refrigerator door and stared blankly at the food, pushed the little button with her thumb and made the light go off and on.

Half an hour passed. Bea, nearly distraught, had grasped her wiry red hair in either hand and was tugging absentmindedly at her scalp when Tom limped out of the bedroom. "There's a lady in there wants to talk to you," he said, jerking a thumb behind him. "She says don't turn on the light."

Bea closed the door behind her. The curtains were drawn. "Come to bed," Toni whispered. But it was not her flirting tone of voice. Bea undressed and crawled between the sheets, noticing that Tom had washed Toni and helped her change into her best satin nightgown. She and Toni weren't much into lingerie, but they each had one nightgown the other loved, for occasions: New Year's Eve, their anniversary, making up. Bea felt a flicker of jealousy that Tom had helped Toni change into *this* gown, but dismissed it as silly and unworthy. *My god, the man changed her and bathed her, wiped her up when she was loose and dug her out when she was impacted.*

"Lay keppele." Toni had learned a little Yiddish from Bea. They cuddled on their backs, Bea's head resting in the hollow of Toni's shoulder. "You know I love you with all my heart," said Toni; with her mouth so close to Bea's ear she only had to whisper.

Yes.

"For so many different reasons."

"Tell me." Bea had both hands folded over her stomach. She rubbed the back of her head against Toni's shoulder like a child snuggling in for a bedtime story.

"Because I dig tough little redheads." Toni felt a little nudge from the dope. *"Sweet* little redheads." She felt Bea purring. "Something else, too."

"What?"

"Now don't be hurt, even if I say it all wrong."

"No."

"How much you needed me. How much you needed to be loved."

"Me?" Bea was nearly forty, ten years older than Toni, and all their friends pretty much took it for granted that Bea was the strong one.

"Baby, you have to trust me a whole lot now 'cause this is going to sound so terrible, but I couldn't even say it now if you hadn't changed, if you were still this way. But the way you were when I met you, you only used to think about yourself, you only used to talk about yourself, everybody noticed it." She felt Bea stiffen: it was the sort of thing you say in a lover's quarrel. "I'm sorry baby—when you're dying you have to cut right through, you don't have time to go around. Just let me finish." She blundered on gamely. "F'rinstance, if someone was telling you that their car broke down, you'd listen for a minute and then start talking about a time when your car broke down. Or even when my father died, you listened for a few minutes and then started talking about your father. *I* knew you weren't selfish. You just needed attention, you needed love, and it was so easy to give you what you needed.

"Poor Bea, my dying is such hard work for you. When you promised to take care of me I thought about you holding my hand and feeding me soup with a spoon. Instead there's catheters and bedbaths and bedpans . . . it never stops . . . and you're always *listening* for me. And, take this afternoon: when you weren't taking care of me, you were helping Anne with Danny. Oh baby, sometimes I think it's the only thing worth hanging around for, to be watching you, seeing how much you've changed." She paused.

"It's not true," said Bea into the dark. "It's still selfish. I made a deal with God. I'll do whatever has to be done, I'll never complain, I'll never ask for more. And in return . . ." She stopped. *In return, nothing. Just this: stasis: Toni's pale blue eyes to see me from time to time: her presence: a warmth: not to be alone again.*

"You jerk. Bea, I'm afraid."

"Baby."

"Not of dying. Dying's easy. I'm afraid that when I'm gone you'll be so hurt and bitter that you'll go back to being that old

Bea and the only good thing to come out of all this will be gone —*poof*—and all our love, my dying . . . none of it will have meant anything. That's worse than just dying." She turned toward Bea, the Chux crinkling under her, and with her fingertips tenderly traced the outline of a nipple. It was a reminder of when they'd first made love: she had stroked Bea like this and Bea had joked about a man who had honked her like a bicycle horn. *Squawnk!* They used to come laughing sometimes, then.

Toni slipped her hand down and with fingers widespread, pressed on her lover's womb, said "Promise me."

"What?"

"You know."

"I don't."

"That you won't go back."

"Let me do you."

"No. I don't need that. I need your promise. That you won't be the old Bea again."

"Oh baby don't you know? I could never be the way I was. Not after you."

"Promise?"

"I promise."

As Toni fell back, Bea turned on her side and put her mouth against Toni's nightgown, kissing the wet spot where her own tears had soaked the satin. She never slept that night; she only watched Toni sleep, and held her, and remembered an old song —something about not making promises you can't keep. *I'll keep it*, she thought. *One way or another, I'll keep it.*

5

Danny gained weight and strength day by day on an appalling SpaghettiO-based diet. By Friday the house and garden that had so delighted him earlier in the week seemed confining. More than anything else he wanted to go to a Giants game, but his immune system was still too weak for him to be exposed to crowds. After a good deal of nagging, Tom promised to take him along to Golden Gate Park, where he went rowing every week, and afterwards to the Big Rec diamonds where they could sit alone on the hillside and watch the Summer Leagues.

His mother dressed him in layers against the San Francisco summer: T-shirt for sun, hooded sweatshirt for ocean breeze, puffy down jacket in case of fog. And the Giants cap, of course— Anne saw it bobbing up and down as the '64 Comet pulled away, and smiled at the thought of Danny so excited he couldn't even sit still.

Anne spent her first free morning in ages strolling from garage sale to garage sale under a powder blue sky, wearing a rose colored top with thin lacy straps; the sun warmed her shoulders. She bought two old cardboard-bound Golden Books for Danny at one sad little sale where a few old clothes and books and a broken toaster were displayed on a madras bedspread, and at another found a gorgeous beige blouse for herself and a pair of neatly patched brown cords for Danny.

She rode the streetcar home. Tom had loaned her his Senior/Handicapped FastPass—she remembered to limp as she stepped onto the car, but hopped off much too spryly and wondered if the driver had noticed. On the way home she passed a white cat sitting so still in a window that she thought at first it was made of china. As she rounded the corner in front of Mr. Abe's store, Anne noticed a blue Chevy parked in front of the Casa with a black man in the front seat who seemed to be watching her intently. When he stepped out of the car, she saw him reach into his inside jacket pocket—it was a process-server's reflex—and caught the white flash of the envelope out of the corner of her eye. She pretended not to have noticed him, but turned casually, as if she had forgotten something, and walked back toward Mr. Abe's. She heard hard-soled shoes against the sidewalk and hurried into the store.

The process-server had palmed her photo—he glanced down at it one more time before she turned: she was thinner than in the picture, but it was her all right. "Miss Dawson!" He broke into a trot but slowed down again when she entered the store. He smiled, opened the heavy wire-mesh screen door, and strolled into the store, transferring the envelope to his right hand. He only had to touch her with it to make it a legal service, and he didn't mind a *little* chase: made him feel like he'd earned his money.

He blinked in the dark of the cluttered store, and his smile faded. He crossed the store in three strides, glowering down each narrow aisle, almost tripping on a carton of paper towels. There was nowhere to hide and no other door, but the damn woman was gone.

———

The boat house at Stow Lake was painted like a log cabin, and the concession stand with its pink popcorn bricks and perpetual orange-whip fountain made Danny think of the circus. The high school girl behind the counter smiled down at him. "Giants fan, hunh?" The time clock made a satisfying ka-chunk when she punched the ticket for their rowboat.

The dock was slick and shiny, the surface of the lake green as marble. The creak of the davit, the metal *scree* of stirrup in oarlock, and the close-tied boats slamming against each other all sounded muffled in the watery air. Danny sat in the bow at first and leaned forward to watch the prow slice through the dark water. Tom was not heavily muscled, but he had a tall man's long-boned leverage, and a powerful stroke. The aluminum boat skimmed over the water, cutting through the tendrils of fog scudding along the surface. When he shipped the heavy red oar blades in the air, the drips seemed to Danny fat and silver as Hershey's Kisses. Tom spread his thighs apart and Danny sat between them, little hands riding the oar handles. Tom held the boy's weak right hand to the oar, and Danny's thin arms were suspended awkwardly. His hazel eyes shone with the green of the lake.

After five minutes, even pretending to row was too much for Danny. He lay down on the stern seat, down jacket for a pillow, smiling dreamily, watching the island that rose up in the center of the donut-shaped lake so wild and harmless Tom Sawyer might have played pirate there. He imagined swinging on a rope hanging from a limb, letting go, flying free, splashing into the dark green water. When they were on the far side of the island, across from the vivid little oriental temple, Danny sat up again. "Tom Straw?"

"Yo."

"Did you know Toni's going to die soon?"

It took Tom a moment to poke his heart back down in its hole. "I guess. Depends what you mean by soon." They drifted under the vaulted arch of the stone bridge leading to the island. The water was dark as Coca-Cola, and Tom's voice echoed in the cool gloom. He realized he'd ducked a communication, and as the boat drifted out from under the bridge into the first patch of sunlight to burn through to the lake that morning, asked Danny how that made him feel.

"A little scared."

"What's the scariest part?"

"What happens next, after you die," said Danny.

"And what's that?" A duck with an iridescent green pate honked hoarsely and fluttered its wings, displaying itself to a bemused seagull.

"They just take you away when nobody's looking and make your bed and it's like you were never there."

————

Anne ducked through the lower half of the dutch door behind the counter of the store—cigarette shelves were nailed over the upper half—and popped into Mr. Abe's tiny living room rather like Alice through the Looking Glass. Mrs. Abe, lying on her back on a plump sofa reading a paperback romance, looked up, startled, her eyes a deep black over a majestically hooked nose and short upper lip. She took the situation in with uncanny speed and sat up. Her feet barely reached the faded olive rug. "You owe somebody mo-oa-ny?" she whispered.

Anne shook her head. "They want to take my kid," she whispered back. The other woman looked around as if for Danny. "He's at the park with Tom," Anne explained. "They want to serve me with papers—court papers."

Mrs. Abe nodded. "Doan warry, dey will never get past Mr. Abe." She patted the sofa. "Come. Sit. We watch 'De Yawng and Restless.'"

"But it's Saturday."

The older woman smiled and tapped the side of her nose confidentially. "Betamox."

One hour and three cups of bittersweet Egyptian coffee later, Mrs. Abe led Anne to the back door, which was at the bottom of a high narrow stairwell. The windows at each landing had been bricked up; three floors above them a small bulb burned feebly. "Your boy pretty sick, hanh?" The warped door creaked—a rhomboid of daylight slanted through—the gray floor was speckled with flakes of old white paint from the door— startled dust motes danced in the sudden light.

"Pretty sick."

"Cancer, hanh?"

"Cancer."

"You want a good prayer for him, you say for him, who knows?"

"Sure."

"Say after me: *Ya Shafee, Ya Khafee.*"

They chanted together for a minute, then Mrs. Abe peeked out to see if by any chance the process server was in her backyard. Satisfied, she motioned Anne through the door. "But what does it mean?" asked Anne.

"Means . . . *shafee* is doctor. *Khafee* is medicine. Means Allah is doctor and medicine both."

"Thanks. Thanks for everything."

"Welcome. Welcome."

Anne had to cross two yards and climb three fences with the Golden Books in her mouth and the new clothes wadded in her hand. She trudged up the back steps of the Casa, locked the back door behind her, and collapsed against it dramatically. *Process servers. Fuckers.* She knew they weren't paid by the hour: he wouldn't camp on her doorstep, but would try instead to catch her off guard in a few days. Suddenly she felt terribly alone, as if somehow Danny were already dead. It was an emptiness she'd thought she'd never feel again after he was born.

———

The sunshine brightened the lake as the fog rolled back out to the Farallons, where it would hover until late afternoon. Rented pedalboats, rowboats, and outboards played bumper cars in a circular stream while joggers fended for running room along the circumferential path. Tom had to keep looking over his shoulder to row through the traffic. Danny didn't mind: it was easier to talk about the man who died in ICU to someone who was looking away.

"Mr. Lipschutz was in the next bed from me. He was really sick, even more than me, so mostly he was asleep, or else I was. But one time I woke up in the night and Mommy wasn't there and I was scared. But Mr. Lipschutz said she'd be right back and don't cry, and he promised to stay awake until she came back. Or maybe 'til I fell asleep—I forget. And after that it was like we were friends. Then one night the nurses came running in and they rolled the screens around him. I tried to stay awake but I fell asleep, and when I woke up the next morning his bed was empty and nobody even wanted to talk about him anymore."

"Was that the time you tried to take your own IV out, and Dr. Hoffman came to see you?"

"That's when. Is she coming back soon?"

"Monday."

"Good." Danny had liked Dr. Hoffman, a short stout woman with bright little mouse eyes, who told him that Mr. Lipschutz had died and didn't need his body anymore. Then she told him a story about caterpillars turning into butterflies, which made him feel good. But another part of him knew that dead people didn't make cocoons but got buried and turned into slimy, drippy things like in the old comic books he'd found in an attic once. That was before he could read even a little, so the pictures were vivid as a shaman's spell.

But those weren't real either: they were comic books, stories like Dr. Hoffman's. All grown-ups seemed to know about dying was stories, and *that* made him feel like that time he fell out of the boat in Clear Lake *and there was nothing to hold on to.*

A fiberglass pedalboat full of Chinese teenagers bore down on them, the driver shrieking with embarrassment as the steering wheel spun freely: a rudder cable had snapped. Tom worked the oars independently and the boats just missed each other, but he was too close to the shore: the prow plowed through the high spear-shaped lilies until the rowboat beached itself gently on a sloping mud bank slimy with duckshit and feathers. Tom let it be; he turned back to Danny. "Kirk to engine room," he said. "What's the damage report, Scotty?" He answered himself: "The faserrr banks arrre doon, Cap'n."

Danny pointed to the receding Chinese. "Klingons," he said, and cackled behind his hand like Ernie the Muppet. An outboard passed near them and the wavelets rocked the beached rowboat softly. Danny felt funny—he turned the bill of his baseball cap forward again and lay back down across the cushions along the stern seat.

"Anyway," Tom was saying, "we don't just take people away and make the bed when they die at the Casa."

"We don't?" said Danny—he'd forgotten for a moment what they were talking about.

"No, we all get to say goodbye for as long as we want." He saw the boy's face go opaque with concentration turned inward. "You feeling okay, Danny?"

"Not really." That meant no. *Really* meant yes. *Oh really* meant I don't believe you.

"Well, we'll head on back." Tom started to rock the prow free, but turned again when he heard a rhythmic thumping. "Tom Straw!" Danny called, as his right arm slammed itself spastically against the stern. "I'm not doing anything," he cried, as if he were going to be punished. "I'm not doing it on purpose."

Tom held Danny in his arms for a long minute, not trying to stop the seizure, only cushioning the boy as he thrashed. When it was over he rowed back to the boat house, where a boat boy in blue coveralls helped Danny onto the dock. Danny was still shaken, but wanted to walk back to the car. He held Tom's left hand for a few steps, but the giant's lurching motion was too much for him and he let go. The sidewalk was stencilled "No Roller-skating"; the trash cans were chained to the green slatted benches. An old woman in a nappy gray overcoat threw croutons from a plastic bag to a dozen fat ducks and one seagull disguised as a duck, wings folded and neck drawn in.

"I still want to go to the ballgame," said Danny reflectively. "But I don't mind so much if we have to go to the hospital first."

Chapter

Tom and Anne slumped over their late supper that evening, exhausted from a stressful afternoon in the hospital. Danny was behaving like a little wretch, but neither of them had the heart to yell at him. Eventually he became absorbed in conducting a Talking SpaghettiOs pageant where the good guy blood cell noodles ate the bad guy germ noodles, but the moral was unclear, as both good and bad alike were gobbled up indiscriminately by the Mouth in the Sky. It was a very angry play. He was so tired himself he almost did a face-down in his bowl, but resisted mightily being put to bed. Finally Anne let him sit up in bed with his pad and crayons for as long as he liked. She returned twenty minutes later to find him nodded out over a drawing of little black bubble-headed figures crowded into the bottom right corner of the page. All of their limbs were disassociated, unfinished and free-floating.

His stubby white fingers were damp and sticky; she took the pad from him; he murmured in his sleep as the head of the bed whirred, descended. His cap had fallen off; Anne bent to kiss him on the forehead. At first his baldness had unsettled her: she found her glance skipping away, unable to rest on his scalp. She couldn't pretend everything was all right in the presence of that obscene expanse of shiny skin, even after the stitches had been removed. Once she'd stopped pretending, though, something in her heart softened when she looked down at him: now that he was bald she could see in his face the face of the infant he had been. She slipped the cap back on him, tugged the bill down tenderly, and went off to find Tom Straw.

———

Tom's bedroom was the smallest in the house. The big bed took up most of the floor space. A dresser was backed against the wall, and books and journals were strewn on either side of the bed. The double-sashed window was opened a crack: a dog barked and a mockingbird practiced a repetitive rising scale somewhere in the valley of backyards. Anne sat at the edge of Tom's bed. He'd pushed up his left pajama leg and was massaging his stump with vitamin E oil. She couldn't look down and wouldn't look away.

"Frankly my dear," said Tom, "I've had better days."

"Actually," said Anne, "*my* morning was going rather well until the process-server chased me." She hadn't wanted to tell him in front of Danny. Her pupils were dark, mischievously wide.

"You're kidding." Tom capped the oil, dried his hands on a towel that lived damply under the bed, and rolled down his pant leg.

"I never kid about process-servers. But don't worry, he never laid a glove on me."

"What's it all about . . . ?" Something in the phrase echoed for both of them: it was an old song. "Alfie," they sang, in unison. Anne smiled at Tom. She had already grown fond of him. His gentle care of Danny had won her heart, and though he wasn't quite her physical type (she'd always liked pretty boys with dark curly hair), in her present circumstances she found size and strength more appealing than ever before.

"It had to be Roger Pierce—Danny's father. I think Dr. Bruner got in touch with him after I refused the next round of chemotherapy for Danny. But he's got no say. Pierce has got no damn say. The only reason he even knows he's the father is 'cause I was temping at his firm then, and I needed to go permanent to get on the health plan. We managed to avoid each other at work until I got the job with the Public Defenders, and up until he got divorced he'd see Danny a few times a year, when he could sneak away from his wife." She shook her head resolutely. "I've never taken a cent from him, his name's not on the birth certificate, there's no *way* he's got any say. The decision about the chemotherapy was mine, and I damn well made it."

"Must have been tough."

"Not really. He'd already been through the 5-FU series, which Bruner said was the best they had and which probably wouldn't make him sick. So he puked his poor guts out and it didn't do a damn thing. And after that, Bruner wants to try something completely experimental, that he won't even *say* won't make him sick."

Anne looked down, found a loose orange thread in the hem of her jeans. She knew better than to pull it and pulled it anyway. Tom found his Swiss Army knife in his jeans, which were crumpled on the floor beside the bed, and unfolded the scissors for her.

"Thanks." The tiny blades snipped. "Look, Tom, I know I said the other night that I knew how all this comes out, but I don't. I really don't."

"Do you *want* to know?"

She looked away, startled, shy. "Just tell me if there's any hope." Suddenly Anne was frightened—she had a fairy tale feeling, as if she'd just called the genie and now she wanted to change her mind, but couldn't. In the stillness she heard the whistle of the wind spilling through the fog corridor over Diamond Heights.

"There's always hope," Tom said. "It's what you hope *for* that changes. We can hope for periods of remissions, for no metastasis, for good weeks, good months. . . ." He rattled on. It was a pat answer. *True,* but pat. It had moved him when he'd first read it in Kubler-Ross, but now, parroting it, watching Anne shake her head wearily, sensing that he was losing her, it sounded merely glib, a pun, a play on the word *hope,* and his voice trailed off.

"Thanks, Tom," said Anne and patted his foot as if to comfort him. Then she leaned over quickly and kissed him on the forehead before he could react.

"Anne," he said, as she started for the door. She turned around. "If the process-server shows up again, let him serve you. If there's nothing to it, we have a lawyer that'll injunct Pierce's ass so fast his head'll spin."

"Thanks," she said. "That would be fantastic." She closed the door behind her. Tom wanted to say something else, to call her back. Then it occurred to him that he only wanted to cheer her up, as much for his own sake as for hers. He sighed, reached behind him for his Walkman, and popped in a bootleg Grateful Dead tape. Dr. Hoffman always teased him about listening to the Dead the way the Christians flipped through the Bible at random, seeking solace or inspiration. It worked, too: the first song he came to was "I Need a Miracle." *Need lots of miracles around here,* he thought. *Lots.*

7

"I didn't know how much I missed this," said Tom on Sunday afternoon. He and Anne were sitting on the hillside above the great emerald bowl of the Big Rec diamonds in Golden Gate Park. Danny had scooted down closer to the right-field foul line. He knew he couldn't keep the foul balls; still he followed them with his eyes, hungry as a retriever.

"Missed what?"

"All this . . ." Tom gestured toward the eighteen-year-olds whipping the ball around the horn, earnest as puppies. "I haven't seen a game since . . ." He tapped his hollow left leg. "It was my best sport in high school."

"I would have thought basketball."

"Heightism rears its ugly head. Just 'cause you're tall, people think you dig running around in your underwear. I was only six-four then, anyway."

"What position did you play?"

"Pitcher."

"Were you any good?"

"Better'n that kid that's throwing now." Even to himself he sounded like an old fart; he laughed. "I got looked at by a couple schools, but nobody came through with a scholarship, so I went into the Navy inst—Good stop! Nice stop!" At the crack of the bat the shortstop had scuttled sideways into the hole; there was a soft puff of dust as the first baseman shifted his feet to catch the throw across his body. "D'ja see that, Anne? Attaway!" Tom leaned back again. The sun was warm; he could smell the ocean. When Anne lay back with her arms at her sides, her hand came to rest in the crook of his elbow.

The inning ended; the players changed sides as the old man who spent his weekends announcing the games droned on through his portable loudspeaker from the stands behind home plate. When a warm-up throw sailed over the first baseman's glove, Danny scurried after it on hands and knees and threw it back. The Redwood City first baseman scooped up the boy's toss and swiped at an imaginary baserunner—"Got 'im!"—and Danny beamed. At the next change of sides the ballplayer stopped to talk with Danny, who then scooted up the hill toward Tom and Anne backwards on his tailbone without taking his eyes off his new hero. Anne sat up, and he backed onto her lap. "He said 'Good arm' to me."

"Well, you made a good throw," said Tom.

"If I grow up I'm gonna be a first baseman, too. He says you get in a lot of plays and it helps if you're left-handed like him and me." Anne hugged Danny convulsively; he wriggled free and scrambled back down the hill.

"*If* I grow up?" said Anne, shaken. "Do you think he knows?"

"Who knows? Even if he does, he may decide to forget again, later."

———

Anne climbed out of the Comet and felt the first push of the late afternoon wind testing the air. It whipped at her legs though the sunlight still glinted off the parked cars across the street. She helped Danny out of the back seat. He was exhausted, but his cheeks were ruddy and his eyes shone. As they walked around behind the car Anne noticed that one of the Comet's taillights was broken and called up to Tom about it. He turned, halfway up the steps. "Yeah, thanks. I saw it yester—look out behind you!"

She spun around as the burly process-server sprinted toward her from the sunny side of the street, round brown head down like a fullback, coattails flapping. She threw up her arms; he slapped her hand rather harder than necessary with the envelope. "Whups, sorry. Thought you was gonna pull another goddammed Houdini on me."

"You got me fair and square," she said evenly. "Now fuck off."

"I hope the boy feels better." He backed into the street, checking his watch to note the time of service, then turned and walked back to his car.

"The fucker was *whistling*," said Anne, later, in the kitchen. She and Tom and Linda Sanchez, who had just returned from a weekend in Stinson Beach, were drinking coffee; Danny had a cup of pale beige, coffee-laced milk.

Tom's chair was tipped back against the orange wall; with his legs outstretched his size thirteen high-tops were half way across the room. "There's some professions where you just shouldn't whistle," he observed. "Process-servers . . . under-takers . . ." He watched slyly as Linda brought her cup to her lips, and said "Proctologists" just as she took a sip. Timed it just right: she laughed so hard the coffee spewed out her nose and splattered the table. Anne ran for the paper towels.

They were still laughing when Dr. Hoffman called from Omaha a few minutes later. She and Linda talked while Tom rode the groaning elevator to the attic to take the call in his office. He flicked on the light in the windowless room, sat down at the desk and picked up the receiver. "Hi, Frieda. How's Omaha, Jewel of the Prairies, Gateway to Kansas?"

"Oh lord, I've eaten so much steak I'll never be able to look a cow in the eye again."

"How did the workshops go?"

"They went well. More nurses than doctors, of course."

"Of course. What time you coming in? I'll pick you up at the airport."

"That's why I called. As it turns out, there is a conference in Vancouver next week. They've tracked me down here and I promised to speak to them tomorrow night and participate in a seminar on Tuesday. So I was thinking that perhaps I'll just fly up there directly, instead of coming home tomorrow morning and having to fly back out tomorrow evening. Can you handle things there until Wednesday?"

"Sure, no problem."

"How is Toni?"

"She's lost a lot more weight. Still tolerating liquids, and managing pain with Brompton's. Some tissue sloughing in the urine. Her spirits are great though."

"And Bea?"

"I don't know, Frieda. I just don't know. We get along okay, we joke, we keep each other at arm's length. Maybe she'll talk to you."

"Maybe. She hasn't yet. But tell me, how is that sweet little boy?"

"Danny's a delight. He got me out to a ballgame today— you know I hadn't gone to one since the amputation. He's another little teacher, that one. He had a seizure yesterday— Bruner adjusted his meds. We're watching him."

"And the mother?"

"Anne? Oh, she's a peach."

"Linda mentioned something about a process-server from the boy's father?"

"That's nothing. I'll sic Michael on the bastard tomorrow."

"On the what?"

"Oh come on, Frieda. He's just harassing her. He's got no chance."

"No chance for what? To see his son? What on earth is the matter with you? Why are you calling this man you don't know a bastard? You're not getting . . . involved with this woman, are you, Tom?"

"No, ma'am," said Tom, whose mother used to tell him that every time he lied, an angel died.

"Good. I mean, life is life, but we have a tough enough job without mixing all that in. My father had a saying . . . how should I translate it? 'Don't fart in the beans.' "

"Your father must have been a very interesting man," said Tom, who wanted to change the subject before he killed any more angels. "Look, this is costing a fortune. Why don't you call me from Vancouver with a number there, and your return flight. I'll pick you up."

"All right, dear. Speak to you tomorrow."

———

When Tom went downstairs to start dinner, Linda asked him what the good doctor had to say.

"She said, 'Life is life and don't fart in the beans.' "

"Oh, was it you who was doing that?"

8

It was a lonesome Wednesday for Danny, what with Mommy at court, Tom Straw up in the office working, and the tv in Toni and Bea's room inaccessible behind the closed door. Hatless, scalp sprouting barely-visible down, Danny watched Linda as she tried on shiny silky slips and prosthetic bras—he took mutilation pretty much for granted by now—and anointed herself with powders and lotions until the room swam with sweet pink smells. Then he wandered down to the weight room in the basement, where he stared up at Tom's weights in their racks. He tried a few sets of forearm curls with the one-pound dumbbells, like Tom Straw had taught him, but couldn't even lift the weight with his right arm anymore, so he instead decided to conduct the World Championship Rolling Dumbbell Race. But the finish line was the wall, and long before the finals Bea had stormed down the back stairs and into the room. "Do you *know* what that *sounds* like up there?"

Danny couldn't think of an answer. He *liked* Bea. He felt sorry for her, too: sometimes he thought she was the saddest person in the Casa, even though she didn't have cancer. He looked up at her, and enough passed between them that her eyes softened and her shoulders sagged. She turned away, trailing her hand behind her for him to take. "Come on, honey, let's go watch some tv. I think 'Diff'rent Strokes' is in reruns in the morning now."

———

Anne met Michael Kantroff, a lawyer who donated his time to the Casa, in front of that unhappy building known for some reason as the Hall of Justice. He was a modern day gentleman: he let her pass through the metal detector first. "That's in case anybody tries to smuggle in some justice," he said and led her down to the dismal cafeteria in the basement. She liked him right off. He was a slight six-footer with a high forehead, honest eyes, and a crooked smile. He wore the obligatory three-piece suit, but not well, and when he stood on line for coffee and donuts she followed the bright bobbing of his red tie through the smoke.

He had her sign the affidavit his secretary had typed up the day before and took from her a photostat of Danny's birth certificate, then led her to a nearby empty courtroom with wooden benches hard as pews. They were early. "I'll meet you here in fifteen minutes," he said. "Don't worry if I'm not back when they start—*jus' rise when de man say rise.* This should be a piece of cake. I never *did* like that sonofabitch Pierce. Even in high school. Did I tell you we went to Lowell together?"

The courtroom was brown, cold and lonesome; the fluorescent overheads were reflected in shiny pools in the dark wood of the counsel tables and the Bench; the flags drooped in their sockets. Anne watched the stenographer set up his machine as a few more litigants straggled in uncertainly. She set her jaw when she saw Pierce and felt the bright spots burning in her cheeks as he approached her. Then Michael appeared and headed him off. The two lawyers shook hands and Pierce whispered something; Kantroff laughed and turned away just as the bailiff sounded the oyez.

"Your Honor," said Michael, rising casually when the case was called. "If I may approach the bench . . . ? I think I can save the Court some time."

It was hard for Anne to hear the rest, but when he had finished, she saw Judge Orster lean forward—he had a very large, very judicial head and a veiny nose—to speak to Pierce's attorney, a plump man who kept jerking at his tie like Rodney Dangerfield. When the clerk called the next case, Michael sauntered back to Anne smiling. She followed him out of the courtroom.

"He thought you'd show up without representation and he could slide right past the paternity issue. The judge reamed out poor Rollie pretty good. Of course now he's going to seek to establish paternity. I take it he's . . ."

"He's the father."

"Fine. Then we'll whip his ass on the custody." Michael flipped a salute to the black guard at the metal detector by the front entrance.

"At the racetrack the winners tip the security," the guard suggested.

"Well here's a tip for you," said Michael. "Go work at the racetrack."

Anne laughed and touched Michael's sleeve; she felt like skipping down the sunny steps. "Can I drop you anywhere? I have Tom's car. Right over there. In the blue zone, I'm afraid . . . I thought as long as it had the handicapped plate. . . ." The traffic on flat gray Bryant Street was orderly as always—too many hungry cops this close to the Hall of Justice—so they both turned to look when they heard the silver BMW burning rubber at the stoplight. Michael pointed. "Isn't that . . ."

"That's Pierce," Anne said, just as Rollie puffed toward them from the street, stuffing the tails of his sweat-stained white shirt into his baggy suit pants.

"Tough to have your boss for a client, eh, Rollie?"

The fat man rolled his eyes. "Look, Mickey, we have a problem. Can I talk to you for a minute?"

"You bet. Just let me have a minute with my—"

"Like, now?"

The two men conferred in the sharp sunlight for a moment, then Michael turned to Anne. "What's the address at the Casa?" he asked with forced calm.

She told them.

"Rollie thinks Pierce may be on his way over there."

Rollie's car was bigger, Michael's faster, but the Comet was closer: Rollie squeezed into the back seat and held on wretchedly to the blue plastic armrest as the car careened down Folsom, past gray steel factories and warehouses big as airplane hangars, cutting along past the Southern Pacific sidings, edging west or south as the right-on-reds dictated. The babble in Anne's mind was like static but she steered the old boat with loose wrists, easing out of a four-wheel-drift of a right on Army Street with her foot still on the accelerator, taking a looping left on Dolores around four of Mother Teresa's nuns crossing two abreast in their blue-trimmed saris, looking down at their sandals, telling their beads furiously. *Holy Mary Mother of God,* thought Anne, who was not Catholic and had forgotten the rest. *And blessed is the Fruit of Thy Loom, Jesus. Oh shit. Sorry, God.*

Then a picture of Danny came into her mind—a fresh picture: bald, bilious, weeping—as the spires of grimy St. Paul's arose before her.

"I'm going to lose my fucking job, you know," said Rollie suddenly. The Casa appeared, white and blue as Mother Teresa's nuns. Fiery red bottle-brush blossoms were mirrored in the polished, elegantly sloped trunk of the silver BMW in the driveway.

—

The BMW had swooped through the sparse morning traffic. *That's just like that bitch Anne,* thought Pierce. She had known damn well he couldn't sue for paternity while he was still married, much less while his already messy divorce was under way: his ex's attorney would have had some fun with *that.* Not that it had been any picnic sneaking away a few Saturdays a year to see Danny. But he'd always told himself that *someday* he'd get to know his son, that *someday* there'd be time.

Then in late May Bruner had called him out of the blue to tell him that Danny was dying and that Anne had refused chemotherapy for the boy, and it had occurred to him that *someday* might not come.

At the thought of how long the prescribed succession of lawsuits would take, and how long that fucking Richmond District Jew Kantroff could stretch it out before he could get Danny back to Protestant Mercy, Pierce felt a sickish swelling in his throat and chest and choked the fat leather-padded steering wheel until the feeling dropped low in his belly where it could burn comfortably as anger.

Big shot lawyer, he thought. *Can't even get to see my own kid. Much less save him.* He was on the right block now—didn't even have to search for street numbers—the big white and blue house all but flagged him down. He pulled into the driveway, set the hand brake, and checked his watch. *Say I got a five minute start on 'em. Time to scoop the kid up . . . then what, big shot?* The car door slammed sturdily behind him. His mind ran on as he trotted up the steps and rang the bell. He noticed that his hands were shaking.

Toni opened her eyes to see Danny at the foot of Bea's rocker watching an odd-looking black boy on the television screen. "Is that a *real* little boy?" she asked Danny. Bea's knitting needles clicked in hypnotic, down-jabbing rhythm.

"Sure," said Danny. "His name's Gary Coleman."

"Oh. I thought he was a puppet or something."

Danny thought that was funny. "He just has fat cheeks."

"Plus I think they messed with his hormones like that poor Michael Jackson," Bea suggested.

Danny looked up. "There was a girl at the hospital named Sami who had posters of Michael Jackson up all over by her bed. She wrote him that she had cancer and how come he always wears one glove?"

The doorbell rang. "I'll get it," said Danny. When he stood up Bea rocked forward impulsively and pulled him in close for a hug.

"Well?" she asked.

"Well what?"

"Well, why *does* Michael Jackson wear one glove?"

"Well, *Sami* says he wrote and told her, but in the letter he said it was a secret and she shouldn't tell anybody." He heard the elevator shudder to a stop, heard Tom Straw's heavy uneven tread in the hall. He finished hurriedly. "But Benjy Wirtz said Michael Jackson only sent her an autograph picture and she's just making it up about the letter."

By the time he reached the kitchen, Tom Straw had answered the door. At the end of the dark Victorian hallway, Danny could see his father and Tom Straw framed in the yellow white glow of the doorway.

"I'm Roger Pierce and I'm here to see my son Danny." Pierce lowered his shoulder as if to push by. Tom anchored himself in the doorway with his left hand against the jamb and reached out to hold Pierce back at arm's length, fingers fanned out across the rough wool pinstripe of the man's vest.

"I understood there was still some question about that," Tom said, neutrally as he could.

"Get your hand off me!" The pigeons on the second floor window ledge were startled into the air by the shout, but settled back down after a moment, huffy and disheveled.

Tom felt Pierce tense up and anticipated him, pushing back lightly, fingers flexing against the lawyer's chest. Then he dropped his hands. "Sorry. Thought you were gonna trespass."

"All . . ." The pigeons fluttered and grumbled; Pierce looked up uneasily and lowered his voice. "All I want . . ." He paused to get his breathing under control. "I just want to see my son for five minutes. Then I'll—" He broke off, staring past Tom to Danny shuffling down the dim hallway toward him. His face drained and flattened in horror like a man in a centrifuge, and he had to turn away.

Tom Straw stepped out on the narrow porch with Pierce and closed the front door behind him as Bea knelt beside Danny in the hallway. She started to hug him, but he pulled away.

"What?"

"That was my father," he said and saw again *that look* that had passed across his father's face before he'd turned away. He'd seen it before, but always on strangers. Danny scolded himself: *I should always, always, always wear my hat.* The pain that wrenched him wasn't physical—it was more like when he thought E.T. had died—but he felt such a pure sweet sorrow for himself that it was okay, it was like feeling sorry for somebody else, and once he started sobbing he couldn't stop.

———

"You okay?" Tom touched Pierce lightly. The smaller man jerked his shoulder away from Tom's consoling hand and fled down the steps. Pierce saw the Comet pull up to the curb and double park, but kept his face averted, and was backing out of the driveway before Anne and the two lawyers reached the bottom of the steps.

"No harm done," called Tom, but Anne heard Danny howling and raced up the steps to find him cuddled in Bea's arms.

"It's all right, honey," she called. "Mommy's here now. It's all right. . . ."

Danny cried himself out on his own bed, with his head cradled in his mother's lap. Then she lay down on her pallet and they napped together while Tom drove Rollie and Michael back to pick up their cars at the Hall of Justice and continued on to the airport to meet Dr. Hoffman's flight.

———

Anne awoke terrified from a long dream in which a hospital had lost Danny: she'd run down shiny corridors under high domed subterranean ceilings, and everyone had been as polite as the Elves at Disneyland, but no one knew where he was.

She came down to the kitchen to find the coffee already made, still warm in the hourglass-shaped glass pot with the wooden collar. Unable to dispel the mist of her dream, uncomfortable with Danny out of her sight, she carried her cup back to the bedroom. She found Danny sitting up in bed. His face was puffy and placid as always, but there was a wildness in his eyes. When he saw her, fat tears formed and fell. He had had a bad dream, too: he wanted to ask her if his daddy would take him away, but knew somehow that if he heard himself say those words it would feel as scary as in the dream, so he said instead: "I hate Daddy just as much as you do," but that was scary, too. He reached out for her; she made room for her coffee cup on the bedside table among the medicine bottles and kleenex and water glass and Donald Duck comics, lowered the side bar, sat on the bed and took him into her arms again. He snuggled his head against her but that wasn't enough. His good hand reached up blind as a kitten and patted her breast as if he were comforting it—*there, there.* When she let him rest it there, a measure of calm spread through him like an endorphine rush. She folded her arms around him and rocked him gently. If she could have, she would gladly have nursed him again.

Late that afternoon Anne dragged two lawn chaises to the sunny patch of lawn at the back of the garden. The grass was a bit ragged, the variegated ranunculus cartoon bright. Danny climbed carefully onto one of the chairs, lips pursed in concentration. He felt the sun's warmth and remembered dimly the heating pads his mother once used for his stiff neck. He picked up the wrist of his right hand with his left and draped it across his body so it would get the full heat of the sun: maybe that would help. He saw his mother watching him. "Good thing I'm left-handed, right?"

It pierced her: it was something she used to say to him way back when the paresis had begun. She nodded. "That *was* a good throw you made the other day."

"You 'member that, huh?"

"Mommies 'member everything good." She adjusted her ragged straw sun hat. "Is your arm getting any worse?"

"No, look, it's better." By twisting his trunk he made the arm flop from the shoulder. His mouth was dry from the medication; he tried to spit. "Can I have a grape?" She found the paper bag in the tote and handed it to him. He liked grapes— you didn't have to peel them. "Can I have the Fritos, too?" He broke a Frito lengthwise and inserted the shard into a grape held between his teeth. He liked the crunchy salty Frito hidden in the tart springy grape. Now he was ready to talk about his dream. "Mom, will Daddy get to take me away from you?"

"Daddy?" She laughed. "Never in a million years."

Danny looked around at the German ivy spilling over the high wooden fence enclosing the yard. "He couldn't get over *that* fence, anyway, could he?"

I did, she thought, but said, "Oh, no, sweetie, you're safe here. Safe as safe can be."

He closed his eyes and eased into a half-sleep, feeling the sun on his face and remembering how he'd thrown the ball *right to* the first baseman, remembering the sweep of the imaginary tag.

But when Anne closed her eyes she heard the dogs barking and the washing machine churning on the service porch next door, and the radio of the house painter up the hill. And when she opened them she saw the star-shaped leaves of the German ivy invading their yard, engulfing the fence and choking the forsythia, and it filled her with an unreasonable anger. She fetched the big hedge clippers from the toolroom and waded into the ivy, relishing the heavy crunch of the steel blades and the feel of the rough wooden handles twisting in her palms. She hacked away, resting only long enough to wipe the sweat from her eyes with a bare forearm and fan herself by flapping her hat, until the dark soft wooden boards were exposed. Knee-deep in the fallen ivy, she felt an absurd urge to stomp it, or whack it flat with the back of the shovel, but settled instead for stuffing it into several leaf bags and hauling it to the garbage. Then she lay back on her lawn chaise, pleasantly tired, scratches stinging, and regarded her handiwork: blackened old boards, blind grubs scurrying from the newly turned earth, and the scarred forsythia trembling like the Elephant Man in the unaccustomed light of day.

Chapter

10

Tom built a small fire in the front parlor fireplace. "In honor of your return," he said to Dr. Hoffman.

"A sensible honor on such a chilly night." She leaned forward in the Chinese-yellow wing chair; he stood behind her kneading her neck and shoulders and discreet dowager's hump. "Thank you, that feels *so* nice. That's the worst part about traveling—no neck rubs."

"You could always hire a masseuse."

"I don't like professionals. You don't know *where* their hands have been." She looked around slyly. "Of course I don't know where *your* hands have been, either."

"Nowhere interesting, alas."

"I don't doubt *that.* You've been living like a monk since I've known you."

"Frieda! Getting a little personal, aren't you?" He rubbed his hands together briskly, pressed his warm palms against her neck to finish the massage, then lay down on the blue and yellow oriental rug in front of the fire. "Anyway, I could say the same about you—you've been living like a monkess."

"Dear Tom, I'm well over seventy, and I am, as a philosopher once said, freed from the grip of that cruel and inhuman tyrant known as sex. You, on the other hand, will undoubtedly wither without a little romance. In fact, as your physician, I prescribe it. Take your young lady out on Friday night. Get to know each other. I'll cover for you."

"You're serious."

"Tom, she's a lovely girl. I take back what I said about farting in the beans."

"Aren't you sort of taking something for granted here? Like, maybe Anne might have a little something to say about the matter?"

"She might indeed." The old doctor winked. "You ask her, Tom. Just ask her."

———

Frieda stayed home, on call, Friday night in the exquisite little dollhouse of a Victorian she owned up on Pacific Heights, while Linda Sanchez babysat for Danny, and Tom and Anne took in a not-very-good movie about the sixties that they both enjoyed inordinately. Every twenty minutes or so one character or another would hop into a car and the soundtrack would blast some old Motown at them quadraphonically: that was all the art that was needed to win them. Later, up on Twin Peaks, looking out over the city and the bay, and the East Bay spread out sparkling before them, Tom quoted Michael Herr: "Just a couple of old rock and rollers with one foot in the grave." In the silence that followed he wondered if perhaps it had been an ungentlemanly remark, but in fact it had been well received: Anne was only watching his face and feeling tender. She edged closer and tipped her face up to his. *If he doesn't kiss me*, she thought, closing her eyes, *I'll look like such an asshole.*

But he did. And then he brought up one hand and placed it under her sternum, palm up, fingers spread wide as a baseball glove, so that when she rested all her weight on him they each felt her heart beat against his palm. It was what she needed: to be borne like that. And what he needed: to bear her up. "Let's go home," she whispered, but kissed him again before he could turn the key in the ignition.

———

The Grateful Dead were singing softly from the cheap portable tape player; Tom lay back and watched Anne cross the room toward him in her ankle-length red Stanford sleeping shirt. She sat on the edge of the bed and with a mock sleight-of-hand flourish held up a joint for his approval. "Do you smoke?"

He smiled. "On special occasions."

"This special enough?"

"It is to me."

"Me, too." The disheveled little room with its scattered piles of books and clothes, the clock on the windowsill, and the tensor light fastened to the wall over the bed with pushpins, seemed close and familiar to Anne, not like a stranger's bedroom at all. They smoked, using a dirty coffee cup for an ashtray, and when they were done she crawled under the covers, and he turned out the light.

She could hear the wind rattling the window and knew that the lights in the valley of backyards would be soft and blurred in the night fog. "I want to make love with you," Anne whispered, "but there's something I have to do first."

Tom waited and waited and then felt her hands on the top of his left thigh; she slid them down until they were around his stump, holding him gently, no pressure, where the truncated bone was closest to the skin. He slipped his left arm around her and felt the tension all the way up her arms to her shoulders. They lay in the dark, barely breathing, for the longest time, listening to the wind, and then her fingers began to move softly, barely stroking the smooth stump skin. "There," she said. "It's all right now. I had to get used to it. But it's just . . . *you*, now." She slid her hands across his long belly and up to his chest and leaned over him. "Hold me like before," she said. "Hold my heart again."

———

While his mother and Tom Straw made love, Danny dreamed of a redwood house under a redwood forest. Ground dark as bittersweet chocolate. Green light deep as the darkest green in the crayon box. He and Mommy and Tom Straw on a porch. "Come inside, we have something to show you." Who spoke? He can't see, their faces are above him. He is in a wheelchair. "I don't mind," he says. "Don't be sad."

From a narrow-railed gallery he looks down at a long room full of people having a party. They all look up at him. Some have glasses in their hands. Linda is there, and Doctor Hoffman, and the kids from Protestant Mercy, and Toni and Bea, and the kids from school, and—there! there in the corner is his Grammy who died and the man from ICU. They smile and nod and point to themselves as if to say: *See? I'm all right. I'm here, too.* The room seems to be built of big Lincoln Logs.

Tom taps his shoulder. "Okay, Danny. Ready for you now." The party is for *him*—he's supposed to do something. He can't remember what, but he knows *why* he can't remember: someone isn't here. Someone important. He beckons Tom, who bends down to him. "My daddy's not here. Would you get him please?"

11

Linda Sanchez tugged her plaid five-wheeled suitcase by its leash; it followed her tamely down the hall to the elevator. They'd thrown a goodbye party for her the night before (nothing much; Tom Straw bought a cake at the zen bakery), but she had refused to say good-bye. "I'll only have to do it all over again tomorrow."

Now it was tomorrow—Saturday—the last day in June. She took the suitcase down to the basement and parked it just inside the garage door, then rode back up to the attic. Tom Straw had his back to the door, copying out her schedule of checkups; a wide melon slice of pale flesh peeked out between his faded black T-shirt and his jeans. She ran her hands up along his back firmly and massaged his neck for a moment. He turned and caught her brown hands in his: huge as they were, his hands made her think of the gawky boy he must have been. He looked her over thoughtfully. "Leaving our Brokedown Palace, hunh?"

It was a Dead song, of course: she knew them by now. "Sometimes I feel like I'm the Brokedown Palace," she said.

"You kidding? You're as good as new. Look, here's the schedule for when you have to—"

"They gave me one at the hospital."

"Better to have it and not need it . . ."

" 'Than need it and not have it.' I will hear that phrase in my dreams."

"Good. So what do you say we get this show on the road?"

"Be a little while, yet. Anne's packing lunch for at least an army and I still have to say good-bye to Toni. We should be ready in half an hour."

———

Toni's eyes were too sensitive for daylight now, so the curtains in the back bedroom were drawn. She spent most of her time asleep, but looked up through her pain when Linda entered.

The Brompton's jello—lime again; a mysterious color in the darkened room—shimmered enticingly on the table beside her, but it was too soon: if she took more now she'd be stoned all morning. "Where are you going to live?" she asked Linda— she'd forgotten.

"Stinson Beach. But I'll come back to visit you."

"When?"

"I don't . . . wait." Linda thought of Tom as she pulled the note out of her purse. "The sixteenth. July sixteenth."

Toni shook her head imperceptibly. "Cielito Linda," she murmured. It was a song she remembered from grade school.

Then a splinter of pain worked its way deep inside her, and Linda's face was gone. Bea leaned over her, looking like her own ghost: bright hair, pale waxy skin splotched like the Red Death from weeping. "Don't be so brave. Eat this." The spoonful of jello, green as the Emerald City, approached.

———

Bea followed Linda into the kitchen. She wanted to get the good-bye over quickly. Life at the Casa de Vida was, after all, full of good-byes. She and Linda embraced; her hug was dry and thin, and when she stepped back her smile did not touch her rabbity eyes. "I'm glad you made it," she said, but there was an ambiguous stress on the 'you' and she turned away, embarrassed, to Anne at the refrigerator. "Take the ice chest if you're going to put mayonnaise on the sandwiches."

"We're out of mayonnaise anyway." Anne closed the refrigerator door with her foot.

"There's a new jar in the second cupboard," said Linda.

"What about Saran Wrap?"

"We used it up on the leftovers last night. Why don't you use the wax paper—there are rubber bands around the doorknob." Linda turned back to Bea, but the quick red fox had already slipped back to her den, to her mate.

———

Toni awoke tentatively, found there was no pain, and opened her eyes. Bea, rocking in the crook of the curtained bay window, knitting relentlessly, was as much a fixture in her restricted line of sight as the white wicker vanity in the corner, or the wedge of pink bathroom counter she could see through the open bathroom door. "Are you almost finished with the afghan?" asked Toni.

"A few more days."

"If you're making it for me . . . I don't want to take it with me. It's too pretty. Pretty things should be here . . . not in a grave."

The rocker paused. Bea tapped the toe of her tennis shoe on the rug as she considered. "That's okay, baby. I was starting to feel like Madame Defarge anyway." Here came those damn tears again—Bea ducked her head behind the curtain and opened the window to smell the flowery air.

"I want to see out, too," said Toni. Bea put the knitting down on the seat of the rocker and crossed the room, took the cheap Woolworth's sunglasses from the night table and settled them delicately on the bridge of Toni's nose. She cranked up the head of the bed and rolled it forward a little, then opened the curtains and stepped back to stand by Toni's side. Together they looked down into the garden where Dr. Hoffman knelt—stockings, good gray grandmotherly suit, cloche and all—weeding around the thorny base of the rosebush.

Frieda had endured a rather unrewarding breakfast with the AIDS Project social workers. They needed beds she couldn't give them yet, and by now something in their eyes reminded her of the relief workers in Vienna trying to get the Jews out after the Anschluss: a seemingly endless supply of Jews, nowhere to put them, time running out, and the death camps waiting.

She stood and brushed the loose dirt from the knees of her stockings. When she sat down on the edge of the green and white plastic-webbed chaise, it folded up on her like a great carnivorous flower. *Oh my*, she thought, pushing up futilely on the rust-flecked underside of the metal bar crushing down on her cloche. *How silly I must look. "Eminent Dr. Hoffman at her Leisure." No no: "Local Woman, 72, Eaten By Chair."* She had to twist her neck around like Quasimodo to look up—the hat slipped off entirely—and out of the corner of her eye she saw Bea, laughing at the back window. When the red hair abruptly disappeared, Frieda assumed Bea was coming to her rescue. She tried to relax; the sun was pleasantly warm on the back of her neck, and somewhere in the city greenery a bird sang as merrily as if it were in a meadow.

Minutes passed—her neck had grown sore—until the back door opened and she heard Bea's sneakers pattering swiftly down the precipitous back steps. "It's Toni," said Bea, kneeling by Frieda's side. The desperate strength in her v. iry arms made short work of the killer chaise. Frieda ducked out and stood, rubbing the back of her neck.

"What is it, dear? Is it the pain?" She stooped for her hat, and Bea literally tugged at her sleeve.

"And she almost choked on the Brompton's. Please, Frieda, for god's sake, hurry."

"All right. All right." Soothingly. "Why don't you go up to the office and fetch the kit? Do you have the combination?"

"Tom never locks it."

———

Toni lay jackknifed across the bed. The flowered nightgown was hiked up over her scant buttocks, and the catheter was tangled between her knees. With Bea crowding her from behind, Frieda put one puffy liver-spotted hand on Toni's shoulder and one on her hip and rolled her easily on her back. "Hello, dear. We're here with you now. Where's the pain?"

"Please." Toni waved a thin hand toward her midsection, then grabbed Frieda's right wrist with all the poor force she could muster.

"Goddammit, Frieda, just give her the shot."

"Bea. Sssh now. Sssh. Don't be afraid. She doesn't have to have any pain," Frieda crooned as she prepared the morphine and compazine. Toni's buttock quivered like a horse's haunch when the needle slipped home.

A few minutes later, when Toni had relaxed into the dope, Bea apologized. "I'm sorry I was such a bitch."

"You weren't a bitch at all. You were a sweet faithful ferocious friend. Everybody should have such a friend when they're sick. Besides, you saved me from that terrible chair."

12

It had been the best day Danny could remember since he'd been sick. *Even including when I could still walk by myself because then I didn't know it would get worse,* he thought, lying in the dark Comet on the ride home across the mountain. He was wrapped securely in a blanket so he wouldn't roll. His right arm lay across his chest (Anne had untied the SpaghettiO-stained sling that hurt his neck); the leg brace kept his useless right foot pointing stiffly at the cracked plastic dome light.

He listened to the car radio awhile—Danny knew lots of new music from the videos on MTV—but when the grown-ups in front punched in a melancholy Jackson Browne cassette, he tuned it out and let his mind be quiet for a minute so he could make his Remember-list for the day.

He'd been making his Remember-lists for over a week. Every day he seemed to feel a little worse, and every night he was a shade more compulsive about registering the events of his day firmly in his mind so that if Tom asked him about, say, last Monday, he could replay it in detail from breakfast (none allowed—tests in the hospital that morning) straight through to bedtime (that was when he got his very own tv that was a surprise present rented for him, and there was cable, too, and he watched MTV 'til late and got so scared from a replay of "Thriller" that Mommy had to sleep in his room all night except she snuck out).

But today had been so full he despaired of remembering it all: the rusty red towers of the Golden Gate Bridge poking up into fat cloud bottoms, the rainbow-mouth tunnel that he couldn't hold his breath all the way through, Tom Straw's games so he wouldn't get nauseous on the twisty highway (chanting thiiis-a-way thaaat-a-way and swaying on the short curves; singing "The Long and Winding Road" over and over for the wide sweeping cliff huggers, where you could see ahead to the next half-mile of coastal highway). And there was Linda's new house with the dark flood stains halfway up the walls and the chickens and the tomato plants, and one of Linda's new roommates who, when Tom asked what breed of chickens they were, said "Sorry-Ass."

And at the beach itself he had seen a Frisbee-catching dog with a kerchief around its neck and an old woman with a white ponytail and a black wet suit going spearfishing. Then Linda's friend Alice had carried him down to the curling tide and let it splash him cold and goose bumpy, and so many people had carried him during the sunset walk that sometimes he traveled with his head cradled softly against breasts and other times lay back against the men's ropy forearms.

Then came the cookout and the stars and the velvet-nosed deer at the Audubon ranch—there was so much to remember, and he was so tired and the long and winding road rocked him this-a-way and that-a-way. . . .

———

Anne snuggled against Tom's side as he drove. She closed her eyes and felt the heavy sway of the Comet through the turns, then sat up to watch the stars over the black ocean. She thought of the Pacific vastness—just the rocky Farallons, then *nothing*—and shivered. "Do you believe in God?" she asked Tom, breaking a long peaceful silence.

"I guess. I believe in *something*—I mean, I *pray*—I don't know if anybody listens—if there's *that* kind of God—but I know there's *something*. And every time I start thinking there's *not*, all I have to do is think about infinity—what's past the universe? more universes? past *them?*—and if it's nothing, what does the nothing exist in?—and there's no answer in *this* world, where everything (he rapped the dashboard twice with his knuckles), where everything is finite in time and space. . . ." He shrugged. "Without *something* else, it just don't compute. It's a dream."

The highway curved away from the coast. Anne reached back to cover her sleeping boy with an extra blanket before rolling down the window to sniff the tang of the eucalyptus groves. "When I was six," she said, "I found my baby book in my grandmother's attic, and the page where it said Baby's first prayer was blank. . . ."

"You said your folks were atheists, right?"

"My mother was what used to be called a lapsed Catholic, and my father . . . my father played the saxophone."

"Oh, right."

"At any rate, as soon as I saw the page was blank, I wrote in my own poem."

"You remember it?"

"Sure. 'Thank you God for the flowers and the trees/ And the butterflies and bees/ And everything Annie sees.'"

"Aww," he said.

She snuggled against him again and rubbed the sleeve of his spotty old suede jacket until what was left of the nap stood up, then drew her initials on it girlishly with her forefinger. "Do you think I should get a punk haircut?"

"Like green or purple?"

"No, not the color. Just the . . ." She fluffed her dark hair into a rooster comb, but it settled right back down.

"Sure."

She had her hand on his right thigh, which was bulked up considerably from almost two years of compensatory double duty; she liked the way the muscle shifted and rolled as he drove. "Tom?"

"What did *your* father do?"

"He was a custodian in the public schools."

"In New York, right?"

"In Newark. There's a lot of dirty water between Newark and New York."

"Straw's an English name?"

"*Straw*'s an English name, maybe. But Straczewski's Polish." They topped the last rise of the Marin headlands to see the city below, shimmering under a bone white gibbous moon. "This is my favorite part of the drive," said Tom.

"I'm glad you stayed awake for it." Anne sat up and rubbed at her eyes gently with her fingertips.

"I only nod out on the straightaways."

"Is that another way of saying the monkey's got the locomotive under control?"

"Absolutely. How's his lordship doing?"

Anne glanced behind her. "Out *comme une lit.*"

"I think that means 'out like a bed.'"

"That, too. I hope we can get him to bed without waking him up." She thought back to when he was little, when you couldn't wake him up after a car ride had rocked him to sleep, and recalled having worried that he'd still fall asleep like that when he was too big to carry. Now, of course, it was not a problem: he wouldn't get too big, and anyway they had his new wheelchair in the trunk.

Damn. There went all the magic of the day like someone had pulled the plug. For the last few blocks, Anne traveled with a sense of unease she couldn't quite pin down. It was only when they came in sight of the Casa de Vida and saw too many lights burning that the feeling solidified, and she remembered how close to death she always lived now, at the Casa. Tom only blew out a long breath and set the emergency brake. With Danny slung over his shoulder he limped across the moon white cement toward the street-level basement door while Anne unpacked the car. Tom left the door open; she closed it with a nudge of her rear end while he summoned and held the elevator. She took her son from him when the cage stopped at the first floor. "See you in a bit," he said. It could only be Toni; Anne could sense him putting on his game face as he stepped out of the elevator.

13

On Sunday morning they held a council of war in the sunny garden, leaving Danny in Toni's room to tap on the window if she woke up. Dr. Hoffman spread the blank nursing schedule on the redwood picnic table. A lackadaisical morning breeze fluttered down the length of the valley of backyards and rattled the paper—Anne found four small stones to weight the corners. Then she stepped back behind Frieda, leaning her chin affectionately on the old doctor's fat shoulder. Tom took the bench across from them; Bea hovered angrily at the end of the table. "This is *totally* unnecessary," she protested. She wore a faded blue and white softball jersey. *"I'll be there.* I'll be there the whole time."

"Of course you'll be there." Frieda reached out to touch her but she jerked away, crossed the lawn with short stiff terrier steps, legs sore from her sleepless night in the rocker, and stopped to pluck a pop-top from the lawn. She stuffed it into her pocket. "But you'll need to sleep," Frieda continued. "If you don't sleep you'll be of no help to Toni or Tom if they need you. And you'll want someone always awake at Toni's side. If she wakes up she may be confused, not able to call out—wouldn't you want someone there? And if she leaves us in her sleep, then someone will be there to call the others."

Tom twisted around on the bench. "Everybody knows you'd take care of her by yourself if you had to, Bea. *You don't have to.* It's not like you're leaving her with strangers or anything. We love her too, y'know."

Yeah, but you can live without her, thought Bea. Tom's long plain face infuriated her; she turned away from them and trotted back up the springy wooden stairs. *She'll just be another old patient you get all misty-eyed about. "Remember old Toni? Boy, was she tough. She hung in there a long time. . . ."* But she stopped at the top landing, confused. "Do what's best," she called down to the three figures around the table in the sun.

When they looked up to her their faces seemed white and very far away. "Just give me the shift that starts now."

They dragged the conference out until the flies were buzzing around the empty, sticky-bottomed coffee cups. "Shift or no shift," Frieda admonished Tom, "you'll have to be close—if she needs injections she'll have to have them. If she lasts past Tuesday, *please* get a relief for yourself. Call Laura—I think perhaps she's ready to come back to work."

"Sure," said Tom. They both knew he wouldn't: the more money he saved on staff, the more he had for nonessentials like Danny's tv. Besides, he hadn't slept more than four hours at a stretch since his tour as a combat Corpsman.

———

Something nagged at Bea all the way back to the bedroom, but she didn't realize what it was until she saw Toni with Danny at her side in his child-sized wheelchair. It was that those three in back—the living—weren't real to her anymore. Not as real as these two. With Toni and the boy it was like being lovers among strangers. Suddenly she flashed on one of the old sixties bibles, Ram Dass's *Be Here Now*. Fat purple paperback. *Boy, we're here now,* she thought. *We're sure as shit here now.*

———

Toni did awaken briefly, later that afternoon. When she opened her eyes the light was broken up into bright patches, violet-shaded prisms at the edges. She looked over at Bea in the rocker by the drawn curtains. "Are you all purple . . . or the room . . . the room is all purple?"

Bea put down her knitting and hurried over. "Thanks for the straight line, honey," she said. "It's just a pigment of your imagination."

"That's *bad*. Anyway, it's gone now." The crystal blur had shattered when Toni blinked away the sleepy tears. She was forgetting the simplest things now—she wanted to apologize to someone. "Just a slip of the eye."

"What?"

"The colors. A slip of the eye. Isn't that a saying?"

Bea corrected her gently: "A slip of the *tongue*."

"Oh." Toni wondered then if maybe dying was just when

you forgot how to breathe. When she breathed next the inspiration was shallow and short of satisfying, and her lungs felt sore, as if they were scraping against her straining ribcage. She wondered how you could think about dying and not go crazy. *Because it's not so scary after all.* She'd closed her eyes again; the darkness was a cold gray.

She must have slept then. When next she opened her eyes the room seemed elongated, tear-shaped, and Bea impossibly far away, back in the rocker in the crook of the bay window. The midnight blue curtains were drawn, but it felt like sunset. "Bea, is it sunset?" she whispered.

"Yes, it is." But it was Frieda, in the wicker chair at her side, reading a *New Yorker* magazine in the dim light, who had spoken.

"How long have you been here?"

"Since four o'clock. Bea fell asleep only an hour ago. How did you know it was sunset?"

"I just knew. I think the pain woke me up. I think if it wasn't for the pain I might not wake up at all."

"Which kind is it?" Toni had her pains named and graded now—this seemed to help her deal with them. "Is it the new one?" Toni had christened the new pain The Alien, which meant nothing to Frieda, but was horribly evocative for those who'd seen that movie.

"No, it's the rolling pain." The rolling pain came from somewhere deep, but referred itself to the ascending and descending colon.

"How strong?" asked Frieda as she prepared the injection.

"Pretty definite. Not rampaging."

"With or without cramps?"

"With."

The rocker creaked as Bea, who'd awakened with Toni's first word, snorted. "What kind of pain? How strong? With or without cramps? For here or to go? Can't we stop playing the goddam games and just take care of the pain, Frieda?"

"We're almost ready," said Frieda, soothingly. She stood and rolled Toni on her side. "But you're right, Bea. What I'd like to do now, if it's all right with Toni, is just give her the morphine regularly, *before* she feels the pain. That is the most efficient

method of all. They swear by it in England. Of course, they have
heroin there—the smaller doses, you know—much more effec-
tive. But we can do it here. Would you like that, Toni?"

"I guess. What do *you* think?

"I think every patient, every person, is different. I need to
know about you."

"Sometimes I feel the one way and sometimes the other. I
think for right now I just don't want the pain anymore."

"You don't have to have it. You have a right to be free of the
pain. A right! That's what I say" (pattering now, to keep the
younger woman distracted while the needle slid into slack muscle). "No more pain for Toni. Never again."

Toni scarcely felt the injection, and the thought that she
needn't fight the pain anymore was as soothing as the morphine
itself. She had Bea pull the curtains so she could watch the
sunset, and the others came in from the kitchen to watch it with
her. And so it was that one of her last coherent sights, with
background and foreground drawn together in customary per-
spective, was the sight of her crew at the window—long Tom,
dark-haired Anne in a fuzzy brown sweater, Danny with his
Giants cap on backwards, the squat strong form of Dr. Hoffman,
and Bea in profile, with her mouth pursed as if for one of her
bitterly funny jokes—and all bathed in a soft amethyst light that
did not hurt Toni's eyes. Behind them lay the cluttered familiar
valley of backyards, the sheltering hillside, and the periwinkle
sky. She would remember the sight in the few days remaining
to her, and even see it in her dreams, except that in her dreams
there was no window: they were part of the bright sunset valley,
and the violet breeze flowed right on into the room, smelling
like heaven, and in the dream the white sheets rustled, then
fluttered and billowed.

———

"We never planned that the Casa should be a hospice," said Dr.
Hoffman, sipping her herbal tea. Tom and Anne were schmooz-
ing around the kitchen table with her late Sunday night, after
her shift. Frieda wore a shapeless gray cable knit sweater and
baggy jeans; her white hair was pulled back into a tight bun and
her eyes were dull with fatigue. "It was only to be a sort of home
care facility for those who needed home and care."

"Until Anker," Tom remembered.

"Until Anker." Frieda smiled, her eyes enfolded by soft wrinkles. Tired as she was, she was in no hurry to leave. The kitchen was just such a nice place to be right then—the orange light had a timeless hearth-side quality and even the hum of the refrigerator was somehow comforting. "Dear Anker." Frieda explained to Anne how the broad-shouldered old man had been down to ninety pounds when Tom, only just promoted from patient to staff, asked him whether he wanted to spend his remaining time on his brother's farm in Minnesota or move to a hospice, either in San Francisco or at Dr. Krebs's up in Bigfoot County.

"I thought he was gonna come up off that bed and slug me." Tom took up the story. "He wouldn't even *talk* to me after that until I fetched Frieda."

"And this man who the night before could barely lift his head," said Frieda, "was sitting up waiting for me and his eyes were big as . . . as that monkey with the big eyes. . . ." She looked to Tom.

He shrugged. "Lemur?"

"As a lemur, then. And he said, 'You told me when I came here that this was my home as long as I needed it. *And now I want to die at home.*' What could I say?" She looked down at her tea as if it had just materialized. "Do we have anything to dunk?"

Anne had just risen to check the cupboard when Bea appeared in the doorway to announce that Toni thought there was somebody else in the room. "She *sees* him. I'm all goose bumps."

Tom pushed back his chair, but Frieda stopped him with an imperiously raised hand. "I'll see to it," she said. "I want to say good-bye again anyway." She had to leave for London in the morning, so the farewell was likely to be their last.

The lights were all out in the back room, but the curtains were open, and the moonlight bled in so dramatically that it felt to Frieda like stepping into a black-and-white movie. Toni's face was Chinese ivory tonight; the unused suction machine squatted under its clear dust cover in a far black corner of the hexagonal room. "So. The gang's all here," Toni whispered fiercely.

"No, it's just Frieda, dear."

"And the others?"

"And Bea. And you're having some hallucinations. That happens sometimes, when we give you so much and so many different medications for the pain. Just hallucinations. They won't last long. And we'll adjust the medications now that we know."

Suddenly, briefly, the old Toni shone behind the deep-shadowed eyes. "Jesus, that's good to know," she said boldly. "I thought I was going crazy." Then she closed her eyes and dropped back into the middle of her dense druggy dream.

———

"When I was a very young doctor," said Frieda, back in the kitchen, "I thought of death as my enemy. Now I think of Her sometimes as a rival. For my friends. Is that too stuck-up? Not that I ever win—at best I can only hope She doesn't set her heart on this one or that, just yet." She carried the phone over to the table and dialed, looking over her shoulder toward Toni's room thoughtfully as she ordered a cab. Then she brushed the donut crumbs from her gray-sweatered bosom and turned back to Tom, waving an oracular forefinger across the littered expanse of kitchen table. "You know, Toni is ready now," she announced.

"I know."

"I think it's only Bea that's holding her back."

"Only for as long as she wants to be held."

Frieda hugged them each good-bye. When the taxi honked from the driveway she picked up her purse, then turned back for a last word. "You know the cancer doesn't want them to die. The cancer only wants them to live—because *it* only lives as long as they do. The deaths are quite unintended. Funny, isn't it?" She turned and strolled down the dark hallway; age had not shortened her stride.

"Do you think she meant funny ha-ha or funny peculiar?" Anne asked Tom. He said he'd known her for years and still couldn't tell.

———

Tom awoke at four without an alarm. He was alone—Anne had gone back to Danny. His left leg stood propped against the foot of the bed; he pulled on a stump sock and leg, then limped down to Toni's bedroom. It was dark but Bea was awake and greeted him. "You don't have to sit up with us. Toni won't wake up, and I can't fall asleep."

"Whyn't you go upstairs and lie down in one of the empty rooms. Anne made Linda's bed up fresh." The round-seated wicker armchair by Toni's head creaked as Tom eased himself down. "I'll call you if she wakes up."

"I want to be *here.*"

"Whatever. I mean, if you want me to go, I'll go. I was just gonna sit here and read awhile, maybe read out loud to Toni later."

"No, stay."

"You sure?" One of his patients had given him a tiny book lamp last Christmas; he clipped it to a fat orange Penguin edition of Nicholas Nickleby and opened it to a dog-eared page.

"You can turn on the light. Look on the bed." She sounded almost enthusiastic; he pulled the beaded chain on the bedside lamp and in its yellow light saw the afghan, finished at last. Toni had tugged it in sleep to the corner of her mouth; with her hair swept up away from her smooth forehead, she seemed serene as a baby with a Linus blanket.

Tom composed his compliment carefully. "It's the most beautiful thing that anybody I ever knew, made."

"You *do* like it." She nodded as though something had been settled. "I finished the last square last night and stitched it together today."

"Where'd you get that purple yarn, that's beautiful."

"Which? Oh, that. That's from a tiny little shop out in the Sunset. They dye some of their own wool. It's the black that sets it off."

"Well, it's gorgeous. I'm glad you finished it in time."

She sat down crossly. "In time for what?"

She hadn't talked about the end yet with anyone. Tom thought perhaps it was time, but Bea turned her back on him, scraped the rocker around to face the window, and leaned forward with her nose touching the glass. It felt good to feel something so hard and cold and real against her face—she was numb to the gut. In the garden the moonlight shone baldly on the lawn.

Here goes, thought Tom. "In time for Toni to see it before she dies. It can't be very long now, y'know."

"No shit, Sherlock."

"Dig deeper, Watson."

The reflection of her wintry smile graced the window.

"Bea, you want to talk?"

"About what?"

"Well, for one thing, about what *you're* gonna do."

"I talk to Toni, sometimes."

"You know you can stay on here for a while, after she's gone?"

"Why on earth do you keep harping on that? In *front* of her, yet." She whipped around and a red-rimmed eye blazed through the bars of the high-backed rocker.

"Sorry. I thought you might . . ."

"Well, I don't." She turned back and watched the red lights of skeletal Sutro Tower blinking over the sleeping city. "Sorry. I'm just so tired." She unfolded her futon alongside the north wall and took the nightgown that had been pressed inside it into the bathroom with her. Tom didn't push it: she had a right to her denial—that was a cornerstone of modern thanatology. A conveniently placed cornerstone, he would think later.

Bea kissed Tom Straw goodnight before she lay down. Loose flannel, then damp lips brushed his cheek; he smelled her Cinnamint toothpaste. He suppressed a silly urge to tuck her in and waited instead for the rustle of her sleeping bag behind him before he turned out the light and turned on his book lamp. The Dickens didn't hold him tonight, though: he soon picked up the bedside copy of Stephen Levine's *Who Dies* and read aloud until both women were sleeping restfully. Then he clicked off the book lamp, scooted his chair around until he was facing Toni, stretched out, folded his hands over his belly and, without ever taking his eyes off the dying woman, fell into a sort of doze, bathing, for a few hours, in the peace that passeth all understanding, without which the art of thanatology is uncertain indeed.

14

Danny passed Independence Day morning in bed watching cartoons, "Sesame Street," Beaver, and MTV. He liked the MTV, liked the spooky dreamscapes of the videos. Never mind that in the real world the sun shone mildly from a high-domed pale blue sky: he couldn't project himself out there anymore, but could only spiral in through the rabbit hole of his imagination, or the tv tube, to find a world that wasn't overwhelming in its sadness, to find a body he could float in, a body that fit the old Danny he still somehow knew himself to be. He had lost heart and needed to be where it didn't feel like he was being punished all the time for something he didn't even know he'd done.

Tom Straw stooped through the doorway to check on him around ten. "Ready to get outta bed yet?" Firecrackers were already popping like small arms fire in the summer streets.

"Not really."

"Let me rephrase that." Tom pivoted awkwardly to duck out the door, then back in again. "Morning, Danny. Time to get outta bed." People were always asking kids questions that weren't really questions.

"Leave me alone."

"Well, I could, as you say, just leave you alone," said Tom in a strangled voice, hunching his head low on his shoulders like a vulture, waggling twin V-signs over his head—he was imitating someone Danny didn't know. "That would be the easy course to follow. But it would be wrong."

"Why?"

"Because"—he reverted to his normal voice—"I went down to the corner of Sutter and Grant at six o'clock this morning to cop *these*"—two fingers long as cigars dipped into the pocket of his black T-shirt and delicately extracted a red tissue-paper packet of Hong Kong firecrackers—"among other goodies, from an enterprising young capitalist of the Oriental persuasion." The Chinatown gates had seemed unearthly stark in the dawn fog. "But we sure as hell can't set 'em off in here, with you in bed."

Danny cocked his head suspiciously. "Could I do some? 'Cause I'm not scared to do it. I was when I was little, though, Mommy said."

"When was that, last year?" Tom teased. He sat down on the edge of the bed and scooped his long arms like a forklift under Danny, swung him in a gentle high arc over his own lap and down into the wheelchair. "You want to go in and wash yourself?" Danny nodded and rolled the one-hand-drive wheelchair laboriously toward the bathroom. "Well, don't forget to wash where the sun don't shine," called Tom; he was rewarded with a chuckle from under the baseball cap. "Your mom's down with Toni—she says come get her when you're ready and she'll make you breakfast."

Shifts didn't mean much anymore. There was no chance of Toni's passing alone: Bea would not leave her and could no more sleep than fly. Tom stopped in hourly, always with a cover errand—some fresh flowers from the garden, a believe-it-or-not tidbit from the paper for Bea—but always pausing to check Toni's thready pulse and shallow respiration. He measured her urine bag around noon, then went outside to help Danny raise a little hell. There was no change in the level when he returned, so he irrigated her catheter. Still no improvement of the flow: it was only the plant, shutting down operations.

———

Danny spent most of the sunny day on a blanket, listening to the poppetypopcrashbang of the urban Fourth, playing with his stuffed penguins, his empty wheelchair standing sentry over him. Outwardly he was placid, apparently detached from the goings-on in the back bedroom. But his penguins had a very difficult afternoon of it, banging heads and squabbling and in general behaving like very wicked penguins indeed.

The wind began to pick up around four. Anne looked to the west, to see if the fog were creeping in to obscure the fireworks display over the Marina, lit a few more firecrackers for Danny to throw, and helped him blow up a dandelion or two. Wanting to shriek, gibber like a monkey—anything to shake off the deathbed constraint she'd been under inside—Anne bellied down on the blanket, seized a stuffed penguin, and attacked Danny. He grabbed another to defend himself, parried, thrust, and struck home to tickle her with a spongy-soft penguin head against her ribs. Then his face was suddenly against hers and nuzzling her softly; his breath was baby sweet again, and his hazel eyes, green as the warm grass, were big and soft-focused as Bambi's. Her heart went out to him with a not altogether painful rush; she gathered him in her arms and hunched over him as if to protect him from the wind.

"Mom?" His lips moved against her collarbone.

"What, sweetie?"

"Let's go see Toni."

And Toni, who had been more or less unconscious for twenty hours, opened her eyes on cue when Anne rolled Danny in. Bea gasped and leaned forward sharply in the wicker chair; Tom swung his left leg off the window seat with both hands, ready to stand, but Toni had nothing to say. She seemed to see only Danny and either smiled or grimaced, then closed her pale eyes again for the last time. And still the thin rib cage rose and fell, rose and fell, buoyant as cork under the afghan of many colors.

———

They bundled the boy in his warmest clothes, wrapped a quilt around him for good measure, and passed him through the window of Eddie Walsh's room (formerly Linda Sanchez's) into the wind and the approaching fog and the incessant explosions cracking like rifle fire or pealing like thunder through the city. The fog had only just appeared over Diamond Heights, darkening the stars to the west; to the north the sky rockets burst like eye candy against a dusty black sky. They sat him on a folding chair, and Anne, and Eddie, a forty-five-year-old union electrician with a treatable form of leukemia, and Stan Peck, the other new patient, gathered in a semi-circle behind him and watched the lights in the sky as if through Danny's eyes. It was an enthralling experience for all of them, and only the cold, and the wet lick of the fog as it reached the flat roof over the service porch, drove them inside again after the show.

———

Toni's last inhale was no different than the others. Her last exhale was longer. No one spoke, no one sobbed, no one seemed to want to move first. After a minute or two Bea stood and looked down at Danny and raised her sparse eyebrows. He nodded his reply; she rolled his wheelchair closer to the bed, and he reached up to take Toni's left hand with his own. He squeezed it as tightly as he could, as if she were still somewhere deep inside her own body. "See you later, alligator," he whispered. Then he let the hand fall back on the afghan, and Tom stooped from his great height to kiss the high smooth forehead he'd bathed so often.

"Bea," he said, straightening up. "You want some time alone?"

"I do," she said, firmly as a bride. "I want the night."

"The . . ." Tom started to protest, but couldn't think why and couldn't get the words out.

She sensed the opening. "Frieda promised I could have as long as I wanted."

He considered as Anne wheeled Danny to the elevator—the boy had fallen asleep in his chair again. Tom was *supposed* to have whoever was on call for Frieda come out to certify the death, but he didn't suppose letting Dr. Chinn sleep a few more hours would cause anybody any undue grief, so he nodded, bent down to hug Bea, and closed the door behind him. He paused in the kitchen to make himself a cup of decaf, tossed in a splash of brandy and a teaspoon of amber honey, and carried it onto the elevator, which clanked and rattled so that he hardly needed to stir the toddy by the time it reached the second floor. He drank it standing up, in his room, listening to the Dead through his Walkman, looking out through the cold glass to the fog-shrouded valley of backyards.

———

The door to the back bedroom was still closed at seven. Tom rapped softly—no answer—and again before pushing it open. His glance flicked from Toni, whose hands were folded peacefully over her belly like a figure on a sarcophagus, to Bea, who lay crumpled on her side at the foot of the rocker. He limped across the room and, kneeling, lay two enormous fingers alongside her neck with an economy he'd learned in combat. The cold, inelastic flesh told him all he needed to know.

He turned her on her back—her face was bluish and slightly deformed by the swelling on the right where the blood had settled. He looked around for something to cover her with in case anybody wandered in. The afghan was folded neatly on the window seat; he reached out a long arm to pull it down. As he spread the bright wool over Bea, he saw the note pinned to it. It had his name on it—TOM STRAW—in tall spidery letters. He slumped back against the side of the window seat and read the first sentence several times over, but it was like reading in a dream. He couldn't concentrate, kept thinking of the unlocked drug cabinet in the attic. Finally he hauled himself to his feet and searched until he found the empty seconal bottle. Thank god it was a scrip from Kaiser, back in October. *He was in the clear.* That's what went through his mind first. Then the shame rose like bile in his throat and he remembered the note, unfolded it again, and turned his back on the suicide to read.

Dear Tom,
 This afghan was supposed to have been for Toni but she said I had put too much life in it for her to take it with her, so she wanted me to keep it, to remind me of a sister who loved me. She was right. I couldn't bear to take it with me either, so I want you to have it, to remind you of two sisters who both loved you very much.

Love,
Bea

P.S. We'd like the Gay and Lesbian Funeral Society to handle the arrangements. They have us on file.
P.P.S. Toni said play Brokedown Palace for her.

Her handwriting had deteriorated with each postscript: there was a third but it was illegible. Tom knew there was a great deal he had to do now, but all he could think was: *loved you very much, loved you very much.*
 He was literally shaking with anger. *Breathe,* he told himself, *breathe,* and inhaled slowly, deeply, blew it all out, and set to work.

15

It seemed as if the fog would never burn away on the Fifth of July. Danny watched quietly through the window of the dusty front parlor as the vehicles came and went: Dr. Chinn's gray Honda and Michael Kantroff's Beetle and the unmarked van from the funeral parlor that backed up to the basement for Toni and the orange and white-striped Paramedic van to take Bea to the autopsy. Nothing cast a shadow in the grayness, and the parked cars had taken on a shiny coat of fog.

The boy had little desire to join the grown-ups in the kitchen: even though they were talking in whispers and their movements were stunned and dreamy he could sense their anger. It was that anger that had propelled Tom Straw through the morning. He'd had to call Frank Chinn, of course, and had the presence of mind to call Michael Kantroff instead of the police. The lawyer had drawn upon the Lowell High old-boy network that still more or less managed the city, and so tunefully were the right strings plucked that both bodies, two teams of bearers, doctors, cops and all were gone by eleven. Too soon, as far as Tom was concerned: by noon he would have welcomed the distraction.

Anne found herself dwelling on the frightening secret that Bea had carried all those hours they were together: what depths there were in a human being, to contain such a monstrous thought so easily. And how alone she must have been, even in their midst. *And in how much pain,* thought Anne. *More than mine? Oh dear god more than mine? Poor Bea.*

———

There was a measured pause on the other end of the transatlantic connection when Tom had finished telling Frieda about Bea. "I see," she said finally. "And otherwise, Toni's dying—it went well?"

"Is that like, other than that, Mrs. Lincoln, how did you enjoy the play?"

"No. I just want to hear about Toni."

"Frieda, we have to talk. Maybe I shouldn't be doing this kind of work, maybe I . . ."

"Yes, dear, we'll talk when I get back."

"Frieda, you don't understand. It was my fault."

"Nonsense, we're not mind readers."

"Frieda, I blew it. I shoulda known."

"When? You should have known when? It wasn't a sudden decision, was it?"

"I doubt it. She must've known . . . oh, a long time ago."

"Then I'm as much to blame as you. And when I get home we can whip each other until we bleed. In the meantime, take care of your other patients."

"Frieda, remember what you said to me when I first wanted to work here?" She had remarked that there seemed to be something in Tom Straw that held back, and that the job at the Casa was a tough one for someone who needed to hold a piece of himself in reserve.

"Yes, I remember," said Dr. Hoffman after a moment. "I was wrong."

"Maybe you weren't."

"Fine. If I wasn't wrong then, I am now. Because now I think you are a fine nurse and I have a great deal of faith in you, which is why I have trusted you to handle things alone more than any other nurse that's ever worked for me. But if you want to have a career crisis, that's all right, dear: you can have a nice crisis when I get back. I used to have them every few years when I first started this work. But for right now, you're in charge there, you're the one that will have to help everyone else get through this. You have patients, Tom. Go see Danny. I'm sure he needs you."

"Frieda—"

"Goodbye, Tom Straw."

"Bye, Frieda." Tom hung up. It was stuffy in the office; he replaced the princess phone in its cradle and turned on the desk fan, then spent a few blank minutes crumpling tiny pieces of paper and trying to throw them through the grill of the fan. He found himself thinking again of the evening he'd asked Frieda for the job. That had been back before the dining room had been converted into a bedroom and was rarely used. The crystal chandelier shed a linen white light; the dining room table had delicate legs like a deer. Tom had sat in the window seat, looking over the black boughs of the winter garden while Dr. Hoffman spoke. He'd recognized the truth in what she said about the part of him that held back, and could offer in reply only a paraphrase of Scrooge to the Ghost of Christmas Yet to Come: "I am not the man I was; I will not be the man I would have been, but for this." For Tom Straw had not been visited by spirits, but in his illness and mutilation had seen his own ghost clearly enough.

Remembering, Tom sighed and rubbed his hands over his face, making an idling noise with his lips. Then he limped down to the second floor bedroom, undressed, and hopped to the bathroom. In the shower, with the water as hot as he could stand, he scrubbed away the morning's adrenaline stink one-handed, hanging on to the highest of the three chrome grab bars in the stall. He was toweling at his lusterless blond hair when Anne knocked at the bathroom door. "Occupado," he called.

"Ah, Señor Occupado. Danny and I were thinking about getting out of the house for a while. Want to come?"

"Where you going?"

"Just cruising."

"Sounds great. Count me in."

————

It had turned into a scorcher of a day once the fog burned off. They drove to Ocean Beach, where heat waves rose shimmering from the Great Highway, seals steamed dry on the gray rocks below the Cliff House, and the sea dashed itself to a blue white mist that softened the horizon past Land's End. By the time they'd reached Golden Gate Park, Tom's despair had been replaced by a feeling that came to him now and again, when things were bad. It had first come to him when he worked the graveyard shift in the burn ward at St. Albans Naval Hospital, reading *Barnaby Rudge* by the narrow beam of a tensor, surrounded by a moaning and a bubbling and the ticky-tacky noises of a hospital at night. It was a sort of groundless confidence that somewhere there was for all of them—Bea and Toni, Anne and Danny, and the Crispy Critters in the burn ward—an end to suffering. Somehow.

———

The table had been cleared and the dinner dishes were soaking in the sink under tiny rainbow bubbles of Joy when Danny had another seizure. It was less severe than the one before. Tom called Bruner's service, and the doctor called back twenty minutes later. They arranged for Anne to check him into Protestant Mercy the next morning for some tests.

Anne slept with Danny that night. Tom lay alone in his big bed and tried to bring Bea's face up from the dark memory sea. When it came (Bea to the life: a Friday night, the Giants on tv, booting a one-run lead in the ninth. Her mobile face twists in a wry and scornful smile, but in her sharp eyes shines a comfortable acceptance: *see: these are our Giants, the wayward children we must love all the more, the more we despair of them*) it came with a lung-searing rush that recalled Stephen Levine's words to Tom: "how painful it is to hold someone out of your heart." And he knew he wasn't angry anymore.

16

Dr. Bruner had left word with the nurses that he wanted to see Anne. The other mothers knew: they left her sitting alone at the round table by the window of the cheerful day room (decorated like a school cafeteria in shades of salmon and burnt orange) looking out over the bay, which was slate blue and flat as a skillet. There had been no fog for three days now. Across the bay Oakland steeped in a tea brown mist; a lone freighter cut a clean, straight wake as it steamed stolidly past Alcatraz toward the Gate.

The room was cool, floating high above the summer heat. Danny sat on the synthetic carpet in his bathrobe and Giants cap, working on his collection of baseball cards—two shoeboxes full—which were currently arranged by team, but had to be re-sorted by position. It was slow, clumsy work one-handed: the rubber bands around the stack kept snapping him. And some of the players played more than one position, which made him feel frustrated and uncertain. He turned his back angrily when his mother suggested he play with something else if he wasn't having a good time. As if he could leave his collection sorted half one way and half the other.

Bruner paused in the doorway to locate Anne, then strode briskly through the room like a movie star avoiding autograph seekers. He greeted her with a pat on the shoulder, quick and comfortless as a cough, and slid into the molded plastic chair across from her. She blinked; his head was haloed with a violet aura by the bright blue glare of the sky behind him. "Sorry to keep you waiting," he said automatically.

"That's all right," she replied, just as automatically.

He glanced down to be sure Danny couldn't hear. "I wish I had some better news for you," he said.

"I know you do," she said, surprisingly. He was a small man with a delicate, neatly angled jaw. It occurred to Anne for the first time that the man was no older than she. As he talked,

Anne noticed a bewildered three-year-old black girl in pigtails and a pink dress sitting at Danny's elbow, sucking her thumb. She was newly arrived that morning, dressed as if for a birthday party. She edged closer to Danny, who twisted around to keep his body between her and the cards.

Anne felt pulled by a sudden silence into restating what Bruner had said. "So what you're telling me is that the treatments *most* likely to help didn't do a damn thing, so now you want to try something *less* likely."

"Would you be happier if we tried the least likely first? Look, Anne, at this point there is no conservative treatment. There's no holding action: we either attack or surrender." Again he glanced down at Danny, whose back was still resolutely turned; he lowered his voice anyway. "I won't kid you. There may be some unpleasant side effects: nausea, vomiting, immunosuppression. Nothing he hasn't been through before. But he's young, and he's still fairly strong. And in some cases like Danny's, in varying doses and combinations, this treatment has retarded tumor growth. Now a month or two down the line, slowing the tumor down may not mean much. But if we move *now*—how can it not be worth it?"

Anne had been watching Danny and the little girl and found herself yearning for her son to make some sort of friendly gesture. But his anger was still jerking him around—his movements were jagged and distracted, and he continued to ignore her. When Anne looked back at Bruner her head felt suddenly clear as the wall of windows behind him. She leaned forward, mirroring his posture. "It can not be worth it if it makes him sick and *doesn't* help him. It can not be worth it if it's something that just has a tiny chance of helping him, but it's like an experiment or a *research* project that you want data on and it fucks up his last summer on earth even more than it's fucked up already."

He looked back into her eyes; a smile parted his thin, neat lips. "Anne," he said, "I know damn well there are oncologists who'll implement procedures without a ghost of a chance to help the patient, just to gather data. There are doctors like that in every field—hell, it's encouraged: those artificial heart circuses are a good example. But I'll promise you this: they don't work for me and they don't work in this hospital." His pager beeped—he reached into the pocket of his lab coat and turned it off, then looked down at his watch. "Shit. I'm due down in radiology twenty minutes ago." He started to rise, then sat back down. "I don't know what to tell you. All I can do is give you my word, as a doctor." He looked up brightly. "Hell, I'll give you my word as a *father*, that there is a possibility of Danny getting some benefit from this treatment. As far as *research* is concerned: it's not a dirty word. I can name you ten kinds of leukemia that were death sentences ten years ago that we can treat now—and that's from research. But I'll give you my word anyway: this is the last long shot I'll ask permission for. If this doesn't work, we'll leave the boy in peace." He leaned back as if a bargain had already been struck. "Now what I'd *like* to do is try it as soon as possible, while it can do the most good as far as the quality of the time he has left is concerned. In the meantime, there's no reason to keep him here. Why don't you take him back to the Casa for the weekend, talk it over with Tom and Dr. Hoffman, call my office on Monday and let me know what you've decided."

He patted her on the shoulder again on the way out. She watched him pick his way among the kids strewn across the carpet, then looked down in time to see Danny wave a baseball card under the little girl's nose. "See this one?" he said fiercely. "This one's a *Giant.* They're the *best.*" She reached for the card. He tapped her on the knee with it. "You can *hold* it," he said, "but you can't *have* it. Okay?"

She nodded; he handed it to her; she held it in both hands for a moment, then solemnly handed it back. He took it, then turned his back to her and picked laboriously through a stack of cards until he found what he was looking for, extracted it with some difficulty and handed it to her. She took it and held it ritually, then started to hand it back. He shook his head. "You can keep that one," he said harshly. "It's a double. That means I have two. Anyway, it's a *Dodger. Yuck.*"

"Dodger. Yuck," the party girl repeated faithfully, but brought the card up to her mouth lovingly, tasted it, rubbed it against her cheek, and was staring at it dreamily when Anne turned away, heart full of tears.

17

There would be moments in the weeks to come when Anne would look back almost fondly to the weekend after her interview with Bruner. In her memory that time of decision would become the lull between storms, which was odd because living it had been pure, cold hell. She and Tom and Frieda had hashed it out until late Friday night and again Saturday morning, until it became clear to Anne that this decision was hers alone. On Saturday morning she and Danny accompanied Stan Peck, a thin-faced law student with spiky blond hair and a terminal liver, down to the Marina Green to fly his kite, and when the boy appeared to have been calmed by the expanded horizons and the sea air, the boats bobbing like bathtub toys on the white capped bay and the kites scattered like confetti across the sky, Anne told him about the new treatment that might help him, or might not, and might make him sick like before.

"When do I have to go to the hospital?"

"Monday." *There,* she thought. *We'll do it. That wasn't so hard.*

But a few minutes later, with his good hand resting on the thrumming string of Stan's kite, feeling it jerk like a live thing, Danny said, "It feels like it's fighting to get free," and she thought about that all day Sunday. And on Sunday night she went to bed thinking she would refuse the treatment, awoke at two in the morning thinking again, pulled on her robe and wool slipper-socks and went down to the kitchen to heat up some milk. As she stood at the stove she heard, over the hum of the refrigerator and the hiss of the burner, a sound that pricked up the fine hairs on her arms. She turned down the burner and waited, breath held, heart thumping painfully, until she heard again the undeniable creak of Bea's rocker in the back bedroom. The adrenaline surged; she grasped the lapels of her robe tight over her chest. Then she thought of Bert Lahr as the Cowardly Lion twisting his tail—"I *do* believe in spooks I *do* I *do*

I *do*"—and she laughed at herself as Frieda appeared in the doorway in her robe and nightgown, her hair in a loose white braid, an eccentric red tam keeping her crown warm.

"Frieda. I forgot you were staying over." Anne turned back to stir the milk. A skin had already formed; she skimmed it, tasted it absentmindedly, and decided she rather liked the rich burnt flavor. "Want some warm milk?"

"No, thank you." Frieda sat on the red lacquered ladder-back chair. "How are things?"

Anne shrugged as she poured the milk from the saucepan into a fat teal blue mug, and carried it to the table. "I dunno. Did you ever have any kids?"

"No."

Anne sniffed the warm milk steam as she considered. "Frieda, it's worth it. Even now, knowing what's coming . . . it's still worth it."

"Oh, we all have to believe that, dear. We *have* to."

Then she knew. All at once Anne knew. "Frieda, I can't let him go yet. In my heart I can't let him go."

"You've decided, then."

"I guess I have." She drank her warm milk and went back to bed.

———

Mommy. It seemed to Danny that the sickness had dripped into his veins along with the clear liquid, and by the time the drip bag was empty he was full of the sickness, which was the worst he'd known. *Mommy.* Empty-stomached, he retched bile, choked on it and gagged as they cleared his airway and turned him on his side. *Mommy.* "He started before we started the damn drip, almost," a technician muttered. "He's just hysterical."

Hysterical or not, Danny retched at fifteen minute intervals thereafter. Anne held his hand and smoothed his barely fuzzy scalp; she'd been through it before, but this time her face hardened—it was as if she were tempering her will in the horror—and when it was over, she leaned over the boy on the vinyl-padded table as if to protect him with her body, smelling the bile in the shiny catch basin, and whispered, "No more, baby. Never again," as he fell into an exhausted sleep.

They dripped fluids through Danny's IV all night so he wouldn't dehydrate, and when he started drinking again in the morning Anne asked the nurse to remove the IV.

"Oh, I know it must be *so* uncomfortable," said the young nurse, who had doe eyes and a stiff, unbecoming hairdo. She smiled down at Danny in the crisp, freshly made bed. "But I think the doctor thinks it would be better to leave it in than go poking around in his little veins again for the treatment tomorrow." Her eyes flicked over to the clear tubing; reflexively her fingers touched the little plastic wheel that controlled the flow.

"There's not going to *be* a treatment tomorrow," said Anne, feeling cool and thin blooded and heroic after yet another sleepless night.

"Oh yes. Every other day."

"You don't understand: we've decided not to go through with it."

"I see," said the nurse. (Smiling. Smiling. Thinking: *they always pull this crap on the nurse. They never pull it on the doctor. She'll fold when the doctor calls her.*) But when Bruner did call, it was only to ask her politely not to check Danny out for a few more days, so they could keep an eye on him, at least chart the initial effects of the treatment.

"Fair enough," said Anne, who'd been expecting rather more of a battle herself. The two women were punctiliously polite to each other when the young nurse returned to remove the IV, and again a few hours later when she came in to check Danny's vital signs. They were chatting pleasantly about the parking problem in the city when the phone rang.

"Anne? This is Michael Kantroff. If you're not alone, say, 'I think you have the wrong room.'"

"I think you have the wrong room."

"Okay. We've just been subpoenaed. There's going to be a hearing Wednesday afternoon. Pierce is seeking a court order for the chemotherapy—Bruner's testifying it's a life-threatening situation."

"No, not in this room."

"Now Tom's on his way over. He's got something for you to

sign. Then I think the best thing we can do now is get Danny the hell out of there."

"Yes," said Anne. "Yes. No trouble at all. Just call the switchboard, they'll transfer you to her new room."

———

Dear god, how that long linoleum corridor at Protestant Mercy stretched on forever; dear god, how Tom Straw longed to break into a run. He remembered the long stride he'd once taken for granted and tried a step. The right leg remembered how to spring—the arch flexed, the toes pushed—but the left dragged forward too slowly and transmitted the shock straight up to the stump. The pain jarred him clear to the groin. He shortened his stride and gritted his teeth. *Must look like a damn fool,* he thought. *Goddam one-legged stork out jogging.*

He was glad to see that Anne had the bag packed and Danny in his chair. "Let's get this show on the road," he said. "Here, sign this and let's go." He handed her the note he had typed at Michael's dictation. His thigh hurt like hell, but he was pleased that his wind had held—must have been all that rowing.

Anne opened the onionskin paper and read: "On my own responsibility I hereby discharge my son, Daniel Dawson (who is in my sole custody), forthwith from Protestant Mercy Hospital."

"Can they really do this? Make him take the treatment?" she asked, scrabbling in her purse for a pen.

"That remains to be seen. But Michael says if they get a court order while he's still here, he'll have to stay here while Bruner tries to talk a judge into letting him finish the treatment and Pierce gets the paternity tests ordered and the medical records subpoenaed. But if he's already home by then, it's a whole different ball game. Then they have to get an order to take him out of your custody, they have to get an order to get in the house, to take him . . . we can string 'em out." He stooped to push Danny through the wide doorway.

Anne followed with the bag. "But he's *my* kid, dammit. I *do* have sole custody," she said, just before they split up at the intersection of the avocado-colored hall.

"Michael says custody is nice, but possession's even better," said Tom, and he steered Danny left, toward the elevator, while

Anne turned down the right corridor to drop off the release at the nurses' station.

"Mommy," called Danny, frightened.

"Meet you downstairs," she said. "Don't worry." And then, naturally, "See you later, alligator."

"After awhile, crocodile."

"Mañana, iguana," said Tom Straw.

Danny laughed. *Good old Tom Straw,* he thought. *Good old Tom.*

Chapter

18

" 'Mañana, iguana?' How long have you been saving *that* up?" asked Anne that night, seated on the pink shag toilet seat cover in the bathroom appended to the downstairs bedroom. Tom lay soaking his sore stump in the only bath in the house he didn't have to squeeze into; still his right knee jutted high above the herb green water like a great bony mountain. The pink tiles and white ceiling glistened; bath steam mingled with the cotton-white smoke from the joint Anne was smoking.

"Oh, I've had that one ready for weeks," Tom replied.

"Danny thinks the ball is in our court now. He's going crazy trying to think of *another* rhyme."

"It has to be a reptile, you understand."

"We understand. And we accept the challenge." Anne clipped the roach and stood, turning away from him to take off her robe. She seemed all pink and white to Tom as she hung her robe on the back of the door, and wide-hipped and womanly-awkward as she stepped sideways into the tub, steadying herself on the rim. Tom lifted his right leg to make room for her and she lowered herself into the hot water as Tom watched through half-closed eyes. Something had happened that afternoon that had moved him: on the drive home from the hospital, Danny, in the back seat, made a clowny barfing noise, and Anne had turned instinctively to try to catch the vomit in her cupped hands. It was such a perfect mother's gesture and had touched Tom deeply, so now when he looked over at this woman in the tub with him he saw something heroic and mysterious in her mother's body, in the depth and readiness of the love she carried so easily. And suddenly he wanted her, he wanted a piece of that love: a surge of sexual desire coursed through him.

Anne, of course, saw only his hard-on at first. She slid forward in the tub, skin flushed to a pink glow from the bath, and to a deeper goose-bumpy red between her breasts from sudden, reflected desire, and soon their bodies were slapping together happily, and in that closer embrace she felt the emotion that had impelled him and sensed that something had changed between them. And she felt a loosening, an opening of heart, of breast and belly. She stopped riding him and somehow shifted her pelvis so they were bone to bone, deep and still, and as she came she heard the echo of his moan and knew, subconsciously, *what* had changed, and that it was all right now to say *I love you* right out loud. So she did, and right out loud he said, "O god I love *you* . . ."

"I know," she said. "I know."

"I *do*. But if I don't sit up soon I'm going to drown."

Never mind the stupid jokes, Tom Straw, thought Anne. *We know what we know.* They slept together in Tom's big bed that night for the first time in what seemed like a long time. Just before they turned out the light Anne went down the hall to check on Danny.

"He looked so sweet," she said when she returned. "I remember when I used to look down at him that first year or so, when he was sleeping, or lying in his crib discovering his hands or watching his mobile, and I'd think 'How can such a beautiful being come from a horror like Pierce?' "

"It *is* a puzzlement."

She climbed into bed and pulled the comforter up to her throat. "Do you think we could put out a contract on him?"

Tom shook his head. "It's like the Plotnick Diamond, I'm afraid."

"The what?!"

"Didn't I ever tell you that one? There's these two showgirls, Trix and Bubbles, and they haven't seen each other for ten years, and they bump into each other on the street and Trix is wearing a diamond ring with a stone as big as your fist. And Bubbles says, 'Oh Trix, you really scored this time,' and Trix says, 'I guess. But this is the Plotnick Diamond, and it comes with the Plotnick Curse.' Bubbles says, 'What's the curse?' and just then this short, fat, repulsive, warty guy with a smelly cigar comes drooling up the sidewalk and Trix points to him and says, 'Plotnick, kid. Plotnick.' "

"Very funny," said Anne. "But Tom, what the hell are we going to do? Can they really take him away from me?"

With the cool rustle of the cotton sheets against the comforter Tom lay back to consider, hands behind his head, elbows out like wings. Anne felt she could not *bear* the long silence that followed. She sat up cross-legged and draped her half of the covers over her like an Indian blanket; she felt an unreasonable urge to pound on his chest with the side of her fists. His eyes were closed. "Noooo," he said at last, drawing out the word. "Not if they can't find him."

19

Danny slept until noon the morning after his rescue from Protestant Mercy and awoke to find Stan Peck at his bedside instead of his mother. He was fond of the jittery blond law student (and impressed by Stan's former night job as a proofreader in a downtown law factory: Danny knew what "proof" was, and pictured Stan and his colleagues sitting up all night in dim cubicles, searching through fat law books for the *proof*, man, the *proof!*). "Are my Mom and Tom in jail?" asked the boy.

Stan was startled. "What? No."

"Oh. I dreamed they were in jail."

No, thought Stan. *Not yet, anyhow.* "No, they had some errands to run, and they wanted to let you sleep."

"What kind of errands?" Kids have a nose for dissemblance: Danny was on the trail.

"Oh, just *errands* errands," Stan mumbled—he and Tom had agreed that morning that the less Stan knew about the plan, the better. "Tom had to make a few phone calls." Not that the plan was much of a secret: Stan himself had hinted openly that if *he*, for instance, were going away and didn't want *somebody else* to know where he was going, *he* for damn sure wouldn't call where he was going from his home phone where there would be a record of the call that might later be subpoenaed and traced.

Danny was not to be so easily sidetracked. "Why? Is the phone broken?"

Stan felt a little like Lucy Ricardo trying to lie to Ricky. "I don't know. In any event, they said you could stay in bed this afternoon if you were tired, or you could be in the wheelchair. It's strictly up to you."

"Stay in bed."

"Fine. Let me get a washcloth. Do you need to pee?" He helped Danny sit up and pull down his Star Wars pj's, then handed him the carafe.

"Waitaminute," said Danny, taking off his Giants cap. "Is my hair still on?" He was afraid the treatment had caused his new fuzz to molt.

Stan, who had his own hair still, cut in a spiky Reform punk, nodded. "Still there. Didn't they tell you? That treatment yesterday was just a hair restorer."

"You're teasing."

"Yes, of course."

" 'Cause if it was," Danny joked weakly, "I'd rather be bald."

———

Some big shot's Mercedes was parked in one of the handicapped spots near Civic Center Plaza. Tom parked next to it just as a black-and-white rolled by. "Hey Sarge," he called, "How 'bout writin' this one up?" He gestured to the Mercedes.

The cop laughed. "You going to come walk the beat with me in Hunter's Point if I do?"

"Not me." Tom unshipped his crutches from the back seat: he had an ugly blood blister on the side of his stump. *Gotta get me one of those new jogging legs,* he thought. *A nice Off-Road leg with heavy-duty Monroe Air-Shocks.*

Michael Kantroff was waiting for him on a bench in the Plaza, which they referred to as Invasion of the Body Snatchers Park (the remake had been filmed there), a peculiar slab of space, with its rows of twisted lop-topped trees and rectangular reflecting pools wherein brown refugee kids from the Tenderloin splashed, and one rheumy-eyed derelict waded tentatively with his trouser cuffs rolled high. For lunch Michael had purchased a hot dog from the nearby cart—his rather eclectic practice often took him to City Hall or the nearby Federal Building —and the Plaza was a good place to have meetings that he would just as soon not have noted on his calendar.

———

When Tom had finished laying out the plan (they were interrupted once by a panhandler. "This round's on me," Michael said grandly, reaching into his pocket for a quarter), the lawyer shook his head gravely. "As an Officer of the Court . . ." he began; Tom interrupted with a juicy Jersey raspberry. "Formalities having been duly dispensed with," Michael continued smoothly, "and I'll deny I said it to my dying breath: run for it. I think we could hold them off, but it would be a bitch of a time. Anne would be in and out of court. And god help us all if the media got wind of it: that would be a circus for fucking sure."

"And when it's over?"

"At worst, *assuming* anybody still wants to prosecute, you cop a contempt plea and everybody walks. If I can't get you and Anne to walk on *this* one, I'll do the time myself."

"You sure you're a real lawyer?"

"You betchum, Red Ryder. A *real* lawyer'll promise any damn thing off the record."

———

Armed with a pocketful of change, Tom called the Krebs Hospice up in Bigfoot County from the phone booth in front of Mr. Abe's. Krebs himself answered the phone. "Krebs, this is Tom Straw. How's business?"

"They're just dying to get in. How are you?"

"With any luck I'll be able to tell you in person. But look, I'm calling from a pay phone so I gotta make it short. You got room for a five-year-old boy and his mother?"

"Yeah, sure. It's the boy?"

"Yeah."

"What's he got?"

Tom told him.

"Long stay?"

"Who the hell knows? I don't think so."

"Well, we've surprised you before. Look, what's the bottom line? Another MediCal? I lose five hundred a month on MediCal."

"That's what makes you a saint among doctors, Krebs: you're the only M.D. I know besides Frieda who would've asked that question last instead of first. The answer is no, they've got a nice insurance plan, but there's a couple problems. First, you *may* have to carry 'em for a while, on account of there might be some people who we don't want knowing where to find them."

"Long as my ass is covered. What else?"

"Remember how you said you'd always have a job for a nurse who could reach the top shelf?"

"Not to mention somebody I can do Soupy Sales schtick with."

"Soupy Sales schtick?"

"I thought I told you not to mention that! Sure, I'd love to have you. But Tom, the payroll's a little soft 'til late fall. I can give you room and board and petty cash, though, and a nice fat check in late October, early November."

"That'll work."

"And may I presume you and the mother are . . . a Woosome Twosome, as Earl Wilson used to say."

"You may."

" 'Cause I've got the Mickey Mantle Suite open." Krebs was, alas, a Yankee fan: it was his only major moral failing in Tom's eyes. "It's got a bed for the kid and a sleeping loft for you and Mom. When do we see you?"

"Stat. Frieda's going to take over here. She can get the woman I replaced to come back part-time, and if we take some AIDS patients, the AIDS Project has funding—they just need the beds."

"We haven't got any up here yet, but it's just a matter of time."

"I hate to leave Frieda, of course, but she says she can handle it."

"Frieda could handle the black plague. In fact, I think she did. Look, if she gets stuck, have her give me a call—I've got a couple leads."

"Krebs, you're an angel. See you soon."

"The backgammon board will be set up."

"Shit, never mind the salary, then: I'll win yours."

———

"I'm lookin' over my dead dog Rover/ He lies on the bathroom floor." Danny sang the song he'd learned from Tom Straw. "One leg's broken, the other one's lame/ Dum dum dum dum/ He got run over by a railroad train." He could have been singing the Bastard King of England as far as Anne was concerned: it was just so good to hear him chirping again. He was having a good time helping her pack: she'd given him charge of the checklist, and as he still didn't quite have the hang of his new electric wheelchair, he was whirring around the room, in and out of the bathroom and up and down the hall to Tom's room banging off walls and into furniture like a bumper car (and like a bumper car, sometimes he jammed himself into a corner and had to call for help), marking with a purple crayon the list clipped to the board on his lap. He'd been a little ball of fire ever since Anne told him they were going to move. It wasn't that he didn't love the Casa: he only wanted to be as far away as possible from Protestant Mercy.

Even steady Tom Straw seemed to be enjoying the intrigue. He limped into their room after dark and peered through a chink in the blinds at the street for the longest time like a lookout in a gangster film. Anne asked him if he saw anybody watching the house, and he shrugged. Didn't matter: they had decided to proceed under the assumption that Pierce suspected they were up to something, and was having the boy watched. It was all very chesslike, thought Tom, and you couldn't count on luck in chess: you had to plan your moves in advance and *anticipate* your opponent. If they *were* being watched, he had reasoned, they couldn't very well just lug all the suitcases out to the car and drive away. On the other hand it might look suspicious if he suddenly pulled the Comet into the garage on Tuesday evening. So late Tuesday afternoon he pretended to be having engine trouble and had Eddie Walsh help him push the car into the garage. Once inside he backed right up to the elevator, and he and Anne loaded the old Detroit cruiser up to her very gunwales.

The Casa felt strange to Danny, then. He could scarcely bear to look at the patches on the wall where his posters had hung. It made him think of the downstairs room after Bea and Toni's stuff had been moved out; it was as though he were already gone. And suddenly he felt very frightened, lost and alone. He knew his Mom and Tom and Stan and Eddie and Frieda were all nearby, but when he thought about cancer and dying it was like they were all lost and alone together.

He wasn't even aware he'd begun sobbing until he saw his mother's frightened face before him—"What is it, baby, what's wrong?"—and of course he couldn't say. He lifted his good arm and she snatched him from the chair and crushed him tightly to her. Over her shoulder, through his tears, he saw Tom Straw's worried face, white as cauliflower. "What's the matter Danny?" Couldn't talk. "Do you hurt?" Shook his head. "Danny!" Sob. "Danny!" Sob. *"Danny is anything wrong?"*

Is anything wrong? Is anything wrong? Danny seized on the question with a child's mastery of the absurd. *Stupid stupid stupid,* he thought, with a disdain of such intensity that he quite forgot to cry.

Tom got it. "Dumb question, huh?"

Danny nodded. Snot and tears stained the shoulder of his mother's sweater.

"Everything's wrong, hunh?"

Nod.

"Well, you know, when everything's wrong, there's only one thing to do."

Danny was curious in spite of himself. "What?" he whispered grudgingly.

"Order in some pizza and watch the Giants on tv." And spread a blanket like a picnic on the floor of his room and make up funny names for all the teams in the National League, from the Philadelphia Philthies to the Houston Ass-Trolls, and stay up as long as he wanted and fall asleep across the foot of Tom's bed.

He awoke briefly when his mother carried him back to his own bed. His pajama top had hiked up; she lifted him easily in her arms and bent her head to nuzzle his warm belly.

20

Operation BugOut began the next morning under a sky of brushed pewter when Tom Straw gave the order to synchronize watches. This took very little time, as he was the only one of the three who wore a watch. "Sergeant," he called to Danny.

"Yes Sir?" With his round face and backwards cap Danny looked a little like Leo Gorcey, but the goofy grin was pure Huntz Hall.

"You check that checklist?"

"Yes Sir!"

"Doublecheck the doublecheck list?"

"Yes Sir, Yes Sir!"

"Well then let's get this show on the road."

Stan, Ed and Frieda rode down to the basement with the three refugees. Ed helped Anne strap Danny into the backseat harness he'd designed while Tom stowed the wheelchair beside the boy. They all hugged each other then, and wept, and dried their tears before Stan opened the garage door. It all had to be very casual of course—no public gesture of farewell.

Frieda and Ed rode back upstairs; Stan followed the Comet out of the garage and swung the door down behind him. "What time you getting back?" he called loudly, for the benefit of the Unseen Watcher, in whose existence none of them quite believed, or dared to disbelieve. He didn't hear Tom's reply. *It doesn't matter,* thought Stan sadly. *They're not coming back.* He hadn't paid much attention to good-byes before his cancer. Now each one tugged at him a little harder than the one before. He didn't know what it was going to be like to say good-bye to his *old* friends if parting from the *new* ones felt so bad. *Probably tear my heart right out by the roots.* He trudged up the steep white steps slowly, shaking his head. *I'm trying to understand,* he thought. *I'm trying.*

Twisting in his harness, preoccupied with the Unseen Watcher, Danny was a study in manic concentration, frowning every time a car followed them for more than a block. Nor did he relax until Tom took evasive action through Golden Gate Park: a loop around Stow Lake, then a U-turn at the Buffalo Paddock, where they watched the shaggy humpers snort steam clouds in the chilly fog until the road was empty in either direction. Then Tom sang out: "We shook 'em, boy, we shook 'em," as they pulled away.

"We sure, sure did," said Danny, and, free of Protestant Mercy forever, he relaxed against his harness and was peacefully asleep before they'd reached the Golden Gate Bridge.

The sun broke through on the far side of the Waldo Grade; the prosperous pastel valley of eastern Marin glowed in the oblique light. The sky smiled, but not for Anne, who was a saturnine presence riding shotgun. Tom played the clown for her. He joked and told her Krebs stories and played Dead tapes until she pictured herself tearing the tape deck out from under the dash like Wonder Woman and flinging it, torn wires hanging, out onto the highway.

They drove north through the morning, past vineyards fat with July grapes, through softly rounded, lion-colored hills. The tape deck was silent at last; the Comet had settled into its smooth highway stride. "Want to hear a joke?" asked Tom.

"Not particularly." *And quit clowning.*

"Okay, here goes: there's these two prospectors, Joe and Moe, and about halfway across the desert Joe's burro drops dead. And Joe says, 'Oh my god,' and he's wringing his hands, but Moe's smiling. He says, 'Joe, don't worry, we got another burro, we'll just distribute the load, no problem.' And a couple of miles on, the other burro drops dead. Joe's cursin' and swearin', but old Moe's smilin' away. He says, 'Hell, the water the burros woulda drunk, now we can drink it, we're even better off than we were before.' So Joe takes some gear and Moe picks up the water bags and canteens and they trudge on, but after a few more miles they get set on by robbers that steal all their gear and all the water except for one canteen. And by now Joe's pissing and moaning and gnashing his teeth, but old Moe's grinning like a Cheshire Cat. And Joe says, 'What the hell you so happy about?' and Moe says, 'Well, they didn't have to leave us any water, they coulda killed us. Instead we're alive, we got enough water to make it out of here, of course I'm happy.' And just then the canteen springs a leak (Tom made a popping noise with his forefinger inside his cheek) and the water runs out of the canteen—glugluglug—and Joe dives for it and licks up a few muddy drops before it all runs into the sand, and he looks up—they're finished now—with tears in his eyes and there's old Moe . . . you guessed it: there's old Moe smiling. And Joe says, 'How could you possibly be smiling?' and Moe says, 'So what else could go wrong?' "

Anne exploded. "Jesus Christ, Tom, is that supposed to make me feel better?"

Tom leaned away from her, raising both hands from the wheel in a brief surrender; the Comet held the road. "All right, all right. I know I have a strange way of looking at things. Just one more thing, then I promise I'll shut up, I won't say another word all the way to Bigfoot."

"Or play any more Dead?"

Tom agreed reluctantly, then glanced over his shoulder to make sure Danny was still asleep. "There's this line I keep thinking of—I can't remember it exactly—something about how when you don't have anything, you don't have anything to lose. Well you've given up your job, your career, to take care of Danny, you gave up your apartment. And now you have to give up your home again, your friends, the city. You've given up everything except a suitcase of clothes, all for Danny, and you *know* you're probably gonna lose him. . . ." He had the grace not to say the rest. She said it for him in her mind: *So cheer up. What else you got to lose?*

Cute, she thought. *Very cute. Even cuter than Plotnick. He flipped me with my own weight . . . sort of a spiritual judo.* To her annoyance she found a smile sneaking up on her—*Old Moe* —and decided to let it stay there. *Strictly on a trial basis, y'understand.* Then she made up her own joke: *How many clowns can you fit in a Comet?*

As many as you need. She reached into the tape box on the bench seat and selected a Dead tape at random.

Tom looked down in surprise when the music started, then

back at the road. *Not so dumb as I look,* he thought happily. *Which is a lucky thing.*

The Dead were singing "Not Fade Away" on a bootlegged concert tape from the old days when the band would take a song wherever it wanted to go, and for as long as it took to get there. In this case they took the old Buddy Holly song halfway to Bigfoot County, by which time all that was left of it was the Willie-and-the-Hand-Jive beat, and the title being chanted by a voice somewhere far off-mike. "Not *Fade* Away, Not *Fade* Away." Anne found herself chanting along, and when she looked over at Tom she could see his lips forming the same words.

Even after the chant died away, Anne found the words going through her mind—Not Fade Away, Not Fade Away— effortlessly as a mantra, while in another part of her mind Tom's question still echoed: *What else* you got to lose?

"Everything," she said out loud.

Tom looked over, startled. "What?"

The tape ended with a click. "You asked me what else I had to lose," she said, not angrily. "The answer is everything. Same as you, same as everybody." The highway narrowed to two lanes, and dipped through a quiet redwood grove. "It all fades away, Tom. What doesn't fade away?"

"I don't know," he said, glancing over his shoulder at the sleeping boy. "But I have the feeling we're gonna find out."

Chapter

21

Danny opened his eyes just before the highway curved back toward the Coast at Miller Bay, the Bigfoot County seat. He'd slept for hours, but was wide awake now, and Anne took him up front on her lap so he could spot animals—any animals—horses and dogs, mostly; a cow or pig here and there. But when they came in sight of the ocean the boy called wildly, "Whales. Sea Lions. Otters."

"Where? Where?" Anne feigned excitement.

Danny pointed to the gray Pacific. "In there. You can't see 'em but they're there." Then, of course, it was open season as they drove inland again and the coastal brush fields gave way first to hardwood, then dense green coniferous forest: "Bears! . . . Bobcats! . . . Sasquatch! . . ." They all took turns, and the watchword of the last leg of the journey became: "You can't see 'em but they're there."

Twenty miles from the coast they turned off the county road and followed a well-paved driveway that climbed a quarter-mile through one of the few first-growth redwood groves in this part of Bigfoot County to have survived the logger's axe. The Krebs Hospice, built as a hunting lodge back in the twenties, consisted of a dozen redwood cabins scattered on the hill behind the two-story main lodge under a canopy of feathery redwood boughs. Fallen needles carpeted the ground and rolled in drifts over the asphalt walks that connected the outbuildings; the smell was pure piney heaven.

Dr. Krebs himself hurried down to the parking lot below the lodge to greet them. He was a slightly pudgy six-footer with a wide satisfied face, round-lensed, rose-rimmed glasses and sandy hair that rolled back from his forehead in close even waves, and when he smiled at Anne he reminded her of a ginger cat she'd once owned. Danny was hyper but exhausted— Krebs led them to the Mickey Mantle Suite (suite being purely a courtesy title), one of eight that ringed the second floor of the lodge, connected by a four-sided gallery/balcony open to, and overlooking, the Common Room below.

The Mantle Suite was a long narrow room: the white-washed round-cornered plaster walls were of one piece with the high whitewashed ceiling; a hospital bed sat in the middle of a hardwood floor; a high sleeping loft ran the width of the southern wall. While Tom and Krebs helped Danny get settled in his new bed, Anne climbed the ladder to check out the view from the loft through the long horizontal window just under the eaves. Glorious: forest below, strip of blue sky above. After the men had gone she tucked Danny in and pulled the sling chair up to the bed.

"What do you want for your beddie-bye book?"

"Dennis the Menace."

"Again?"

"I *like* Dennis the Menace."

"I bet you do." She tugged affectionately at the bill of his cap.

"No, but I like it best when Dennis is trying to do something . . . helpful for Mr. Wilson or his Mom but it gets all goofed up anyway."

"Do you feel like that sometimes?"

"Yeah. I like his pajamas, too." Anne handed him the comic book, and he flipped through it with his good hand to show her the picture of the Menace kneeling for his bedside prayers.

She glanced at the drawing. "Dr. Dentons? You used to have Dr. Dentons when you were a baby. Red ones—trapdoor, feet and all. God, you were cute."

"I guess they're too babyish for me now or something, hunh?"

She caught the wish in his voice. "They *are* kind of snuggly, aren't they? No, they still make them in your size. Maybe we can have somebody check out the Sears in Miller Bay." She leaned forward to tidy the covers around him again. "Do you want to say some prayers like Dennis?"

"No."

"Okay." She kissed him. "Don't read too late, now. I'll be right up there."

Danny watched her climb the ladder, then listened to her rustling around in the sleeping loft for a while, trying to reassure himself that she was still in the same room with him even though he couldn't see her. Just to be sure, he called her name. "Mommy."

"What, baby?"

Yup, right up there. But as long as he had her attention . . . "Will I really get to ride . . . what was that horse's name?"

"Thalia."

"Will I really get to ride Thalia."

"I told you: if Dr. Krebs *really* promised."

"He really did. He said Wally would take me. Who's Wally?"

"The orderly. I haven't met him either."

Anne found herself humming "Like a Rolling Stone" as she made up the bed in the loft; when it was done she flung herself face down, arms spread, into a nest of comforters that fluffed up around her. Gravity pulled her down like a lover, and she and Danny fell asleep about the same time and slept right through dinner. He dreamt of galloping Thalia faster than the clouds, she of ordering lobster in a restaurant. The waiter set her up— bib, shellcracker, melted butter and all—but the lobster was still alive and spiny angry red and it scuttled off her plate and across the white tablecloth.

She was surprised when she woke up to see through the long low window that night had fallen. She knew she should go down to the Common Room to hang out with the others, but experienced a wild reluctance to join them. *Maybe if I wait 'til later all the dying people will have gone to bed.* But it was such an absurd thought that she jeered at herself—*this is a hospice, for chrissakes.* She made sure the buzzer was in place by Danny's left hand in case he woke up and, leaving the door to the suite ajar behind her, walked down the open gallery to the staircase that spiraled dramatically to the Common Room below.

———

Krebs, who was chronically understaffed, put Tom to work that night after supper, nursing a dying logger in the Yogi Berra cabin. "You should really talk with him if he wakes up—fascinating old guy—*great* stories about Miller Bay and Bigfoot before . . . before the flood, I suppose."

"Did they have a flood up here?"

"Noah's flood. He's ninety-seven. But he's still full of piss and vinegar when he's conscious. 'Hadn't been for this goddam cancer,' he says, 'I'd a lived to be a hunnert, got a tellygram from the President.' " He walked Tom up to the cabin and introduced him to Leah, a dark-eyed nurse with a sweet disposition, a fiercely hooked nose and straight dark hair she could sit on if she so chose. She'd already prepared Jarvis Jackson for the night, so there wasn't much for Tom to do but clip the book lamp to *The Pickwick Papers,* and read, and wait. Just another bedside for Tom Straw, another patient on the border between sleep and coma, coma and death. The square redwood cabin had yellow curtains open to the night, to the grove, which seemed to Tom to be every bit as noisy as the city at night, what with the crickets and flying squirrels, the bats and the pumps and the thump of the moths bashing what few brains they'd been blessed with against screens and lamps and windows.

The evening wore on for Tom. When he noticed a fresh spiderweb in a corner of the ceiling, he was grateful for the distraction. He wrapped some kleenex around his hand and thrust it into the web, twirled the gossamer around his hand like cotton candy until he had reeled in the spider. "Outside for you, Charlotte," he said aloud, and opened the top of the double-sashed window to shake her out. Then he swiped at the last threads clinging to the walls and ceiling, and tossed the kleenex into the wastebasket.

"Two points," said the old man in the bed.

Tom turned around, startled. "Hi. Thought you were asleep."

"You're a new one."

"Yup."

"How tall're you?"

"Two hundred three, two hundred four centimeters." Tom had a lot of wise-ass answers for *that* question.

"What's your name?"

"Tom Straw."

"Not Jewish?"

"Polish."

"Krebs is Jewish."

"I know."

"He's a good man, though. A *damn* good man. Jews musta changed since I was a kid."

"Yeah, well we've all come a long way," said Tom. The old logger nodded off again; his lower jaw dropped open in a curved pink grin. Tom reached down to wipe a thread of saliva from the corner of Jackson's mouth, then settled back down in his chair and opened his book again.

———

Mr. Jackson's heart began to fail toward the end of Tom's shift. He contacted Krebs on the intercom, and the doctor and Wally and Wendy Wane, the head nurse and Krebs's girlfriend, hurried up the path to be with him at the end. Tom went to bed—it had been quite a day—but on his way out Krebs asked him if Jackson had regained consciousness at all.

"Oh yeah, we had a nice little talk."

"Did he *say* anything? Any last words?" Krebs collected last words.

It was an interesting moral problem for Tom, who remembered all too well Jackson's literal last words: he thumbwrestled with his conscience for a moment and won. "He said you were a good man, Krebs. A *damn* good man."

22

Anne was still asleep when Tom climbed down from the loft the next morning, but Danny was half-awake and somewhat cranky, so Tom swung him up to the loft to cuddle with Anne. When he returned from his shower the two were sitting up in bed playing an antique "Mork and Mindy" game that Anne had unearthed from the toy chest downstairs. Tom felt a giddy warmth at seeing them so cozy; he eavesdropped tenderly on the game as he strapped on his leg and dressed, and before he left climbed up to kiss them each good-bye as carefully as if he were Daddy leaving for the morning commute.

Tom took his coffee out to the patio behind the lodge, where a half-dozen round aluminum tables with umbrella holes in the center were bolted to the concrete deck. The light under the redwoods was cool dappled lime.

"Mornin', Jersey," called Krebs. "Pull up a chair. You have breakfast yet?"

Tom lifted a red plastic folding chair from the stack against the north wall of the Lodge. "Mornin', Maynard." (Old nicknames: the two had known each other since Navy days.) "Coffee'll do me—I don't generally eat breakfast." It was cool on the patio; the sun had not yet topped the redwood rise to the east.

"*Ought* to. It's the most important meal of the day. 'Eat breakfast like a king, lunch like a prince, dinner like a pauper.' "

"Adelle Davis said that, as I recall. Just before she croaked."

"What few people know," said Krebs, "is that it was *breakfast alone* that kept her alive the last ten years."

They bantered for a few minutes—each grew lonely sometimes for another east coast wise guy—until Tom had finished his coffee. Then Wendy, the plump blond nurse with the Peter Pan haircut, took him away for his official orientation while Krebs made morning rounds unaccompanied. Then, after they had breakfasted, he took the Dawsons on the Grand Tour.

—

"How did you get into . . . this end of the profession?" Anne and Krebs were following Danny's wheelchair up the paved path that led around the cabins and through the woods toward the upper meadow. They had already visited the creek and the footbridge and the Arts and Crafts cabin, the Viewing Room and the kitchen and the stone well.

"Well. For one thing, somebody has to do it, and most doctors can't. For another, I can't think of another field with more patient contact, which is what I got into medicine for in the first place." The path split around a stand of red-barked understory manzanita: Danny went left and the grown-ups went right and they were gloriously reunited on the far side. Krebs stooped to greet Danny. "Dr. Livingstone, I presume." They shook hands gravely, left-handed. The redwoods, thinning to second-growth up here, maintained a staunch vertical against the slope of the hill, but already Krebs could feel the hazy gold high-summer heat hovering over the meadow. He let Danny roll ahead of them and continued. "And the rewards pop out at you from completely unexpected places—you'll see with Danny. Me, for instance, after three years I still get a kick out of taking visitors around. Some of them come up expecting . . . you know, a *hospice*—people lying around waiting to *die*—and by the time they leave they admire us for the way we *live*."

The vegetable garden made Anne itch to be down on her knees in the dirt with the tomatoes drooping dusty red from their stakes, the fat snapbeans and bushy basil, the sea green watermelons and bumpy-skinned cukes growing together on hillocks, vines tangled. Krebs proudly showed her the gravity-feed drip lines and sloped drainage; she knelt to plunge her hand in the dark topsoil while Danny whirred on ahead to the fenced-in pasture. Thalia, the old chestnut mare, ambled over from the one-horse stable to check him out. He had stuffed loose granola into the left outside pocket of his wheelchair arm at breakfast when he thought his mother wasn't looking. Now he fed the horse through the weathered rails; her soft nose nuzzling at his palm tickled him so funny it stiffened his little peter —he fed her handful after handful until his stash was depleted. "Next time I'll fill my *hat*, too," he promised. He had asked

Krebs again about riding her—first question of the morning—
and had been reassured that someday Wally would take him for
a ride.

And though he was wiped out by the end of the tour the
only way Anne could get him into bed was to remind him that
by the time he woke up the legendary Wally might well have
returned from Miller Bay. Danny *willed* himself to sleep as if it
were the night before Christmas.

———

Mr. Jackson's instructions for his own funeral, dictated to
Wendy Wane in mid-July and witnessed by Leah, had been
characteristically terse: "Don't care about the body. Burn it.
Have Krebs say something. Don't care what. Make sure he
mentions Jesus, though. Wally and me already picked out the
song."

The service had been scheduled for late afternoon, but
Wally had so many errands to run in Miller Bay that he didn't
get back to the hospice until after dinner. It was still daylight
when the staff, relatives, volunteers and mobile patients gathered in the redwood-panelled Common Room, but the sun was
behind the hills and the air smelled of evening. Krebs stood
with his back to the flagstone fireplace and led them through a
hundred repetitions of the Gnostic Prayer of the Heart: "Lord
Jesus Christ, Son of God, Have mercy on me for I am a sinner."
"If you don't think you're a sinner you don't have to say that
part," he offered, glancing around the room. "Just rustle your
wings."

Twenty-some voices murmured for a quarter of an hour.
When they were done a satisfying silence had descended on the
room, and the sky was tinged with violet. "There," said Krebs.
"That ought to be enough Jesus even for Jarvis Jackson. Only
thing I have to add is something I ran across in a Sufi book the
other day: Death is the tax the soul pays for having had a form
and a name." He laughed. "Death and taxes, death and taxes.
Now Wally's got a song he and Jarvis worked out, and he won't
even tell *me* what it is."

"It's supposed to be a surprise," said Wally, who wore his
white orderly uniform, as always. He carried his guitar up to the

fireplace, slung it over his neck and checked the tuning with his back to the others, then turned, double chin tucked shyly into his chest. Against his white-clad bulk the guitar seemed small as a ukelele, but he fingered it nimbly enough, strummed a few chords with his thumb, and sang "The Frozen Logger" in a pleasant baritone.

Anne sat beside Tom on the end of one of the two nubbly-white sofas that faced each other across a low burl table. She knew the song: it had been one of Danny's cradle songs. Danny, beside her in his wheelchair, looked up and grinned and she was glad she hadn't confined him to his room, despite his having spent dinner, as Tom phrased it, "Exploring the possibilities of infantile regression as a vehicle for self-expression," which was to say he hadn't *quite* spit out his just-one-bite-of-Veggie-Surprise-and-if-you-don't-like-it-you-don't-have-to-eat-it, but had only let it dribble out. He'd *considered* spitting it out—Tom had seen it in his eyes—but the thought that he would soon see Wally for the first time had tempered his mischievous urge.

Nor was Danny disappointed when Wally stood up to sing: the orderly was a large gentle-eyed man who looked like Babe Ruth and knew the funny song about the logger who froze to death, which was one of Danny's special secret songs that he thought only he and his Mommy and the man on the record knew. He began to sing along—his mother joined in and Wally looked up. His eyes met Danny's. *Hello again,* he thought, though he'd never seen the boy before.

23

It didn't take Anne long to get the rhythm of the hospice. And Krebs was right: there were times when she'd never felt quite so *alive*. It wasn't any of the nonsense that men spouted about war and football, either: no drama, not even with occasional death. More like a pageant, each summer day passing in slow parade march, but bright and busy as a parade with detail and color and the isolated memorable moment. So Danny would be there for her each morning when she climbed down the ladder, waiting as patiently in his hospital bed as he had waited in his crib when he was a baby (only now Tom would already have washed and changed him and set him up with his book or crayons or penguins), and Tom would be there for her each evening with his long arms and mild loving eyes, and she had rarely been so aware of the ripening of summer or the passage of the moon through its seasons.

On the morning in August when the moon reached full, Anne found Danny in bed with an old hardbound storybook propped up on the lapstand before him. *East of the Sun and West of the Moon.* He showed her the inscription on the flyleaf. "What's that say?" His reading level had taken a quantum leap without a tv, but cursive retained its mystery.

" 'To Joel, Happy Fifth Birthday from Aunt Ruth, April 7th, 1948.' "

"Was this Dr. Krebs's book when he was five?"

"Probably. You can ask him." She untucked him and lifted him into his chair; he followed her out onto the balcony and beat her down to the elevator at the east end of the building. It was waiting for him when he pushed the thermal button: the doors parted as smoothly as if they were on the Starship Enterprise.

They ate breakfast out on the patio with Wally and Fred Small. Fred was a middle-aged man with a creeping neuromuscular disease that had not much further to creep. After breakfast Anne and Wally switched charges: he took Danny up to the pasture in the ATV to feed Thalia; she wheeled Fred back to his cabin to shave him.

"I never shaved a man before," she said.

"I have an electric razor—it's just like mowing the lawn." He turned his head as far as he could and smiled at her as best he could; she wheeled him up the walk to his cabin through the patchwork of shade and slanting morning sunlight, fetched his kit from the bathroom and shaved him on the porch. She found it a more sensual experience than she had imagined: the sharp-smelling masculine lotions, the rough stubble-spikes hiding in the soft folds of his cheeks, the heavy loll of his face between her palms created an almost sexual bond between them. Afterwards she stayed to talk, holding his cold slack hand in hers. Just below the porch a red squirrel scrabbled in the fallen needles; a Stellar's Jay strutted like a blue-combed rooster on the wide redwood railing, jeering because they had no crumbs.

Danny was very mysterious when they met up with him later that morning in the Arts and Crafts cabin that doubled as a library and occupational therapy workshop. "Listen," he said. "Before dinner tonight it's *very important* for me to take a *real long nap.*" His chair was parked under the skylight at a long low trestle table littered with white glue and honey-colored mucilage and balls of yarn and snips of string and boxes of beads, unsorted, and bright feathers and crayons, whole and broken, in shoeboxes, and water colors in tin palettes, and simple wooden jigsaw puzzles with only a few, fat pieces.

"Long nap," said Anne. "Got it. How come?"

"It's a secret." Danny turned back to his glue and toothpicks—Leah had started him on a log cabin. He was supposed to begin laying down and gluing four walls of twenty picks each, side by side like corduroy, to be assembled and roofed later, but he had found the medium rather too confining: as soon as she left he had begun work on an ambitious, free-form porcupiney sort of construction dabbed with smears and tears of white glue.

"Who else"—Fred had to take a breath—"knows the secret?"

"Wally and Dr. Krebs."

Anne wet her forefinger and cleaned a blob of glue from Danny's cheek. "Can I ask them?"

"You can *ask.*"

"Give us a hint," said Fred.

Danny reached out to wipe his hand on a stiffened ball of terry cloth that had once been a hand towel, then reached into the outside pocket of the chair, pulled out the storybook he'd shown her that morning, shook off the granola crumbs and held it toward Fred so he could read the title: *East of the Sun and West of the Moon.*

"Oh," said Fred.

"I see," said Anne. But Danny only smiled, tugged his cap backwards, and turned back to his construction.

———

That afternoon, while Danny napped his crucial nap, Anne and Krebs took a stroll down to the creek. "There's no question he's doing better," said Krebs. The air was deep green and cool; he leaned against the railing of the redwood footbridge and spat meditatively into the trickle of water in the stony creekbed. "I've seen this sort of improvement before—the change in air, altitude, *vast* improvement in nutrition. It could be just a peak —more likely it's a plateau. Too early to even *think* of remission —pray, yes; hope, yes—but don't let's get attached to it. In the meantime we won't mess with success—we'll just keep doing what we're doing, and start him on a program of Mental Imagery as soon as possible."

"What if it was Bruner's treatment, what if that's what made him better?" It was a question Anne had been afraid to ask.

Krebs considered for a moment. "It's not *im*possible. *Anything*'s possible. But it's not very likely. He wasn't doing anything *that* new, you know. And the results he was looking for after part of the first series in *no* way match up with what we've seen. In his wildest *dreams* Bruner never . . ."

He went on, but Anne had more or less stopped listening, except to the trickling water and the breeze fluttering the laurel leaves. Of course she believed him—what choice did she have? Still she resented the assurance with which he swept her uncertainty away. He had been like Bruner in that respect, or like a car salesman: once out of the range of that assurance, she knew, her doubts would come home to her again. Wagging their tails behind them.

———

Danny showed little interest in dinner, which was whole wheat *pasta con pesto* made with basil from the garden. He pulled his chair right up to the lowest table and laid his cheek against the cold aluminum and waited for Wally to be finished. But Wally was never finished until all the patients were finished, and that Mrs. Masur was as bad a space case as Danny had *ever* seen. So he closed one eye, the better to concentrate his mind beam, and thought hard at Wally: *hurry up hurry up hurry up.*

But Tom interrupted his transmission with a glass of water and his vitamins and pills, and Krebs wheeled Fred over, and they all (except Fred, of course) applauded encouragingly for each pill he swallowed.

Then Dave, the cook, who had a ponytail and a long spade-shaped beard like a hillbilly, brought him out a strawberry smoothie that everybody made a big fuss over. Danny knew they were only trying to get him to drink more. *Yummie-yummie yourself,* he thought. They ended up passing it back and forth: a sip for Danny and a sip for Tom, a sip for Danny and a sip for Krebs. . . . Anne went back to the kitchen to get Fred a flex-straw. When she returned Krebs was complaining that he planted the strawberries so he could have fresh strawberry daquiries all summer, and all he ended up doing was feeding the damn birds. "I swear the birds pass out maps, like tour guides—'Free Strawberries at Krebs . . . three stars . . .'"

"Yessir, Captain Queeg," said Tom. Dave offered to substitute hickory bark for the strawberries and make the boss a hickory daquiri, Doc, and as no one was paying any attention to Danny, the boy decided to skip his turns entirely, and just kept passing the glass back and forth among the adults until only a pink froth remained. This he returned to Dave with effusive thanks and an overstated smacking of his cherubic lips. Then he backed away from the table, spun the wheelchair through a stately one-eighty, and whirred away after Wally, who had taken Mrs. Masur back to the Moose Skowron Suite to get cleaned up.

Anne and Fred and Leah were lingering over coffee when

Wally and Danny returned, the latter with a sweater draped cavalierly over his shoulders. "We're going now," he said.

"To east of the sun and west of the moon?" Anne bent to kiss him. "See you later, alligator."

"After awhile, crocodile."

24

Wally went on to the stable to pick up the tack while Danny waited outside the gate. Thalia must have heard them coming: she clopped over from the other side of the pasture and poked her muzzle inquiringly through the fence. In his chair he was not quite as high as her knee; he reached his hand up, palm out, to feel the warm puff of air from her nostrils. There was no breeze in the meadow; the sky was baby-blanket blue. Wally returned and opened the gate for Danny, shut it carefully again. "If you have to open a gate in front of you, you have to close it behind you," Wally advised the boy—that was one of his father's homilies. "Always bridle first: then you have something extra to hold the horse by." That was another.

Thalia took the bit readily; Danny held the cracked leather of the dangling reins while Wally smoothed the blanket over her broad back. "Every wrinkle in the blanket is like a stone in your shoe," Wally admonished Danny, who was flattered to be let in on so many secrets, but said only, "I know," because that's what kids always say when grown-ups tell them things.

Danny straddled Thalia just behind the saddle horn, loosely circled by Wally's arm; Wally rode with the stirrups shortened so his thighs enclosed the boy comfortably and securely as the arms of an overstuffed chair. They sang "The Frozen Logger" as Thalia ambled upward through the thinning timber to the upper meadow saddling the ridge. To the west Miller Bay lay gasping in its customary yellow pulp-mill haze; to the east the Bigfoot Mountains were a jagged purple slash on the horizon. They finished "The Frozen Logger" and began "America the Beautiful" (Danny's version: oh beautiful for spaceship skies). Thalia clip-clopped across the stony golden field; turkey vultures circled gracefully over the northern ridge. When Thalia lowered her head to graze, Danny pictured himself sliding down her neck and laughing.

"See," said Wally. "There's the sun setting in the west"—

exploding into a garish ball of orange and crimson when it hit the rim of industrial effluvium over Miller Bay—"and there's the moon rising in the east." They could just see a thin blue-white top slice of the full moon peeking over the mountains. "So we're east of the sun and west of the moon."

"I know," said Danny. "Can we stay 'til it's dark?"

" 'Fraid not." Wally prodded Thalia gently with his heels and clucked his tongue and she plodded on to the northern edge of the meadow, where he dismounted, steadying Danny with one hand while the boy clung left-handed to the shiny-smooth saddlehorn. Then he swung Danny down and, with the boy in the crook of his left arm like a bag of groceries, led Thalia over to a mountain hemlock. He looped her reins to a nearly horizontal bend in the trunk and admonished her sternly not to eat the needles.

Danny teased him: "She doesn't speak English."

"I know," said Wally. "But I don't speak horse." He helped Danny put his sweater on; they leaned together side by side on a tuffet-shaped boulder, facing south. To the right the sun melted on the Pacific rim; the mud flats glowed in the unearthly light.

"Wally," said Danny without preamble, "do all the patients who come here die?"

Wally considered, rummaging through his homilies. "Dr. Krebs says nobody knows the future. But mostly, that's what a hospice is for. It used to make me feel real bad, but Dr. Krebs says it's like we were working in an airport, and all the patients are just passengers from this country to that, and not to be sad 'cause someday we'll be passengers, too." He hooked his left arm around the boy's shoulders.

Danny looked down at the dark bare forearm hugging his chest and rubbed his fingers over the black hairs. "Make a fist," he said—he liked to watch the muscles stand up. Wally obligingly flexed for him. The sun was soon gone; the moon was full, bone white and hollow-eyed, low in the east, when Danny asked if Wally knew what happens after you die.

"I know what Wavy Gravy says," said Wally. Wavy Gravy was a clown who worked with dying children and ran a summer camp in Mendocino.

"What?"

"He says when your body's so old or hurting or wornout and skinny and it's just no use to you anymore, you'll just close your eyes and you'll see a bright light straight ahead of you and all you have to do is follow the light. If the light goes left you go left and if the light goes right you go right. He says that's all there is to it: you can't miss it and you can't go wrong."

"What happens next?"

"I don't know, but I think you meet a kind friend who helps you."

"Like the Scarecrow?"

"I don't know. Maybe." Thalia snorted impatiently. "She says we better get started back," said Wally. "That's a dark trail at night."

"I thought you didn't speak horse," Danny mocked.

Wally shrugged. "A few words." He carried Danny over to Thalia, untied her reins, lifted the boy up on the saddle, and swung up behind. They started back down the trail; Danny leaned forward to bury his face in Thalia's stiff fragrant horsehair mane; he murmured something. Wally tightened his arm around the boy and leaned forward. "What'd you say?"

"I said you should tell my mother about the airport. She'll like that."

———

The phone startled Tom up from a bad dream that night. He'd been dreaming that there had been some sort of bureaucratic error and the Navy wanted him to finish his hitch. He told them about his leg; they said that was *his* problem. "Yeahello? Hi, Frieda. No. No, you know me, I never sleep anyway. What's—?" He sat up. "Oh God. When? Did it go easy? That's good. Yeah, well it's good you were there." Anne understood then that Frieda was telling him about a death; she too sat up in the dark, pulling the covers up to her collarbone as if an intruder had entered. "He *was,* he *was,*" Tom agreed enthusiastically. "Oh yeah, he'd opened up so much, even in the few weeks I was there. . . ." *Stan,* thought Anne. *Of course, Stan Peck,* and for a moment she was angry at Frieda. *Why did she have to tell us? Don't we have enough death up here?* But she was ashamed of herself: it occurred to her that perhaps death was too heavy a load even for that tough old doctor to want to carry by herself. She threw her left arm across Tom's chest and nuzzled against his side. He pulled her tighter with his arm; she felt his voice rumbling. "Yeah, I'll tell her," he said into the phone. "No, not unless he asks . . . I will. . . . Thanks for letting us know. Bye Frieda . . . yeah, you too." He hung up. "Stan Peck didn't make it," he said.

"Oh yes he did," said Anne. "He most certainly did."

Tom wondered whether his faith was that much more brittle than hers, or if she were just better at whistling in the dark.

25

"Which one are you?" asked the old woman in the double bed of the Moose Skowron Suite.

Tom turned from the writing desk facing the window that overlooked the dark patio with its round empty tables. "Tom Straw, Mrs. Masur."

"Call me Sally."

"Sally."

"What?"

"No, I was just calling you Sally."

"Which one are you?"

"Tom Straw."

"Were you here when I fell asleep?"

"No."

"Am I dying?"

"Not at the moment."

"What are you doing?"

"Writing a letter."

"Well finish up and come to bed." Mrs. Masur smiled; she still had all her teeth. Tom smiled back, tentatively: Sally's memory was impaired, but the rest of her faculties were intact, a combination which made it hard to tell when she was joking. Tom sealed the letter he'd written to Frieda, and after a moment's thought wrote "August West, c/o Krebs" for a return address, then crossed the room to Sally's bedside.

"Why do you limp?"

"One leg." He sat on the edge of the bed.

"That would do it." She patted the empty side of the bed. "Come. Sit with me. Until I fall asleep. It won't be long. I *do* get afraid sometimes."

"Okay, but no fooling around," he said sternly. She laughed. "No, really. You got to promise. I mean, everybody thinks nurses are easy. . . ."

She promised, then reminded him of the old one-foot-on-the-floor rule once supposed to ensure chastity.

"Hell, that's easy," he said. *"I* could leave one foot over by the door."

———

Wendy tiptoed into the Moose Skowron Suite at midnight to relieve Tom and found him sitting up in bed beside the sleeping Mrs. Masur, rereading *Martin Chuzzlewit.* "Aww," said Wendy, for the old woman was curled familiarly against Tom's side. And again: "Aww."

"Two awws?" Tom dogeared his page and looked up.

"Definitely a two-aww scene."

He swung his legs over the side of the bed and stood, teetering for a moment. When he crossed the room to retrieve his letter from the writing desk, he made out two figures down below in the darkness of the patio and the red-orange glow of a cigarette. *Good,* he thought, for he was bored and not at all sleepy. He hurried downstairs (though one-legged men did not *hurry* down the treacherous open-treaded spiral staircase), through the Common Room and out the glass doors to the patio, where to his surprise he saw Anne and Fred Small at a table, sharing a cigarette and a bottle of Green Death. "Hi guys. What's up?"

"We're having a party," said Anne, taking the cigarette from her lips and holding it to Fred's. They were like kids playing grown-ups—neither of them inhaled.

"May I join you?"

"Why, are we coming apart?" said Anne; with her free hand she slid the bottle across the table. Fred's head was turned obliquely away from Tom, face in shadow. Most of the path lights had been extinguished for the night, and the cabins were dark; only the reading light in the Common Room leaked out onto the patio.

Tom took a swig of the bitter ale and grimaced. "That'll put hair on your eyeballs." He slid the bottle back to Anne, who offered to swap it for the cigarette. He declined. "What're we celebrating?"

There was an uncomfortable pause. "Well, that depends," said Anne.

"On?"

Fred stared silently into the dark. Tom tugged his chair between the two of them, farther from the table. Now he could see that the gaunt man was smiling. Fifty feet over their heads a flying squirrel launched itself into the darkness.

"Well, Fred says that you know pretty much when you're . . . when your time . . . when your time is. Is that true?" She looked up to the stars visible through the overhanging branches —it was odd how the clear patches of sky looked like gray clouds against the blackness of the underside of the redwood canopy.

"Oh, absolutely." Tom took the bottle from Anne and tilted it for Fred. "Only thing is"—with the wrist of his sweatshirt sleeve he deftly wiped Fred's mouth, then spoke directly to the paralytic—"you have to be prepared to laugh at yourself in case you're wrong. I mean, don't get *attached* to the idea."

Fred belched weakly. "My daughter's coming down tomorrow. From Portland. I sent for her. She's taking time off from work. If I don't die soon she's going to be extremely pissed off."

There was a hollow hiss as Anne dropped the butt in the empty bottle. "Don't underestimate her . . ." she began.

"No, no. That's why I sent for her. I'm tired. I can't do anything on my own but breathe, and that's worse every day. So I'm thinking, if I send for her . . . if I bring her down here and I *don't* die by the end of the month, she'll kill me for sure."

"Good plan." Tom laughed. "In the meantime, how 'bout some backgammon. I got to practice for the tournament Friday night." He looked sharply at Fred. "You *are* gonna stick around for the tournament?"

"Wouldn't miss it for the world."

26

Danny liked to steer his chair off the path so when it bogged down in the fallen needles it was almost like feeling the softness under his feet. And there was always someone around to get him going again. This morning's game involved the shafts of sunlight slanting through the trees. These were power beams—he had to travel from beam to beam, and if he failed to reach the next beam in time, his ship would run out of power and he would drift forever in the terrible void of space.

From the safety of the patio Krebs and Anne watched the chair lurch from beam to beam. "These are the voyages of the Starship Enterprise . . ." observed the doctor.

"I used to watch Star Trek with my mother," Anne mused. "We had a game: at the start of each show we'd spot all the bit players—you know, the two or three guys you never saw before who'd beam down to the planet with Kirk."

"The ones who always get killed!"

"Right. We'd call them the Expendables, see how many we could spot before they got zapped."

"I swear, we used to do the same thing in my dorm! I'll tell you what, though: I still wish I had one of those little pocket beepers like McCoy had: you just run it across the patient—*wheep wheep wheep*—'oh yes, he has a hiatus hernia and hemorrhoids.'" Then, abruptly, "What do you say we get started?"

"Let's go."

"Hey Kirk! Bones to Kirk, need to see you in sick bay, Cap'n," called Krebs. The wheelchair took a sharp right and disappeared behind a redwood.

"C'mon Danny, we have work to do!"

No answer.

Anne, embarrassed, trotted across the needles; she heard Danny giggling behind the tree and circled it once, slowly enough so he could keep the trunk between them. Then she

reversed her field: "Nyahaha, you've rolled right into my trap!"
She pounced, unbuckled his chest strap and tumbled him forward into her arms and down to the ground with her among the
damp hairy moss and sword ferns and fallen needles, and they
rolled, and it tickled.

"No, c'mon," cried Danny. "Quit. I have to get back to a
power beam."

"No, we have to start the Mental Imagery," said Anne.

But he wanted to play. "No, I'm running out of . . . I'm
fading fast . . . the beams! . . . out of power . . ." And he lay
back in his mother's lap, good arm outflung, only to see Krebs
looming over them.

"I see you've started without me," said the doctor.

"What?" said Anne.

"You see, the first step is to relax."

"I'm not relaxed, I'm out of power." Danny licked his lips;
his eyes were wary.

"Close enough."

"But I want to play." His Giants cap lay just out of reach
against the redwood post that supported the reel for the coiled
firehose. Anne handed it to him; she saw he had his jaw set.

"This *is* play. It's just another kind of play," said Krebs.
"Just close your eyes."

"I don't want to." Danny tugged his cap over his eyes.

"Danny!" Anne was dismayed. "Don't you want to get better?"

"No." He sensed a power over them now.

"What?"

"No. Sometimes I get tired of just always wanting to get
better."

"Well, I don't care. *I* want you to get better."

"Well you *don't* care!"

"Danny!"

"Well you don't."

In the loamy stillness under the trees Anne's heart
pounded; Krebs found the nails of his right hand digging into his
palm. "So much for relaxation," he said. "Danny, what's the
problem? How come you don't want to do this? I told you about
it yesterday—no pain, no needles, no throwing up."

"I didn't say I didn't want to do it. But I was having fun and you didn't even ask me, you just told me just like in the hospital."

Krebs swallowed the crow easily. He had a vision of himself telling this story at the next conference or seminar he attended. He would use it to illustrate how you could learn from dying children. This was not entirely cold-blooded on his part, but only a pleasant idle thought. He said, "All right, let's beam you back to your ship, Captain." He scooped the boy up and held him swinging in the air while Anne, on her knees, brushed the needles from him; Krebs lowered Danny into the chair and his mother fastened the chest strap. They rescheduled Danny's first M.I. session for the Quiet Time after lunch. "You sure that's convenient?" asked Krebs.

"Quite convenient," Danny said prissily—Anne wondered where he'd picked *that* up.

———

Krebs was a bit late—a seventy-eight-year-old man named George Steros had arrived from Miller Bay, comatose, with a naso-gastric tube, and it had taken an hour to persuade his wife that it wouldn't be murder to remove it. Then Fred Small's daughter Emilia had arrived, and he had to show her around and introduce her to Tom. He apologized for not being on time and led Danny through a fairly standard relaxation procedure: close your eyes, imagine yourself on a beach, feel the warm sand, sun, hear the waves, then relax in stages from the feet up. Then he had him visualize the weak confused cancer cells and the strong white cells—Anne thought of Danny's old SpaghettiOs wars. When he sensed Danny's attention wavering, he brought up the boy's lapboard and crayons and had him draw a picture of the cancer cells and the white cells.

Danny's drawings confirmed Krebs's fears: the cancer cells were ferocious, all teeth and three times the size of the white cells, which were huddled together miserably in the upper right corner. He decided to have Wally work with the boy before supper. This meant taking on Wally's workload as well as his own—Krebs rotated his staff through patients, functions, shifts as often as was practicable, limited only by legalities and physiology (in his heart of hearts Krebs thought that only a failure of will kept most nurses and orderlies from being able to function, like Straw and Wally and himself, on four hours of sleep at irregular intervals). All the beds were full and two death watches on, one unaccompanied by relatives. *Ah well, no rest for the wicked,* thought Krebs, and he made a mental note to call in a few volunteers and maybe his backup nurse—Katie West up on the ridge could come at short notice. She'd have to bring her baby, but that was fine—seeing a baby wouldn't do Sally Masur a bit of harm on what might prove to be her last night on earth.

"It's like this," Wally explained to Danny. "You know what cells are?" Danny nodded. They were in the Arts and Crafts cabin. "You know the cancer cells start out like regular cells just like the other ones?" Danny nodded again; with his left hand, the only extremity still completely under his control, he scrib-ble-scrabbled with a purple crayon on the first sheet of a fat drawing tablet. He kept his eyes on Wally, though. "Okay, now pretend like I'm one of your cells," Wally continued, drawing his arms in to look more like a round cell. Danny knew his cells were tiny, microscopic-sized things and laughed at the idea of such an immense one. But he could pretend: he nodded again to show Wally that he'd got it. "And I'm just like all the other cells, except one day I start to grow bigger and bigger . . . and I don't know why . . . and I don't know what's happening to me." He began to gesture with his forefinger, speaking in bursts, growing more alarmed with each fresh catastrophe. "Not only that, I forget how to act—I don't remember how to do my job or anything—plus all your body's defenses start attack-ing me—nipnipnip all around—like piranhas—you know what piranhas are?—so I'm getting attacked and growing and grow-ing and not knowing anything or remembering to do anything. . . ." He stopped. Danny held his breath, his eyes fixed upon Wally's dramatically upraised finger. "Now," said Wally. "How do you think I feel?"

"Like dog poop!"

"You think I feel big and strong and ferocious?"

Danny shook his head. "Boy, I feel sorry for you," he said, but a wolfish grin said he didn't feel sorry at all, and he found himself very much looking forward to his next session of M.I.

27

Fred Small had always assumed death would creep up on him at the same leisurely pace as the paralysis. Despite the assurances of the staff, it seemed to him there was still plenty to fear in such a death—would it be like suffocating or drowning?—but at least, he supposed, there'd be no pain.

He was wrong: When the embolism lodged in his right lung during the Friday night backgammon tournament, the pain stopped him in mid-inhale. As his head slumped forward on his chest he heard the fire crackling in the stone fireplace and the crickets on the hill with their endless Cratchit Cratchit Cratchit. Then Wally, who had been throwing the dice and moving the pieces for him, had unstrapped him and eased him to the floor. He tried to breathe in again—no go—the pain held him firmly in a perfect, not entirely unpleasant suspension. It was hardly even pain if he didn't try to breathe, and the apnea he experienced was not so much like suffocation as it was like a bright light, a blow to the head. Then the light narrowed to a beam, a circle, a pinpoint. . . .

It took them all by surprise: Tom even forgot himself so far as to drop to one knee, upsetting the backgammon board, to start mouth-to-mouth. He looked up, startled, when after a moment Krebs's hand on his shoulder tugged him back from the body. Everyone seemed to be looking at him; in the sudden stillness he heard one of the backgammon draughts still rolling across the hardwood floor—click click click—into the corner; he was embarrassed and glad Krebs had said nothing. Tom and Wally found themselves sitting on the floor; the body in the snazzy pajamas lay face up, eyes and mouth open, stubble dark against bloodless cheeks, between them. *He didn't stop me because it was too late,* thought Tom, dazed—he'd had that happen to him in Nam—*but because it wasn't.* He thought, not for the first time, that maybe hospice work wasn't for him, then noticed Danny had rolled up behind him and was looking down at Fred. "Can he see?" asked Danny. It seemed odd to Tom that the only voice in the room should be a child's piping.

"No," Tom replied, "not with his eyes," and with his right thumb he closed the lids, the jaw.

"Can he hear?"

"Not with his ears."

The news had traveled like a shock wave through the hospice, where sudden death was only a little more common than it was anywhere else. The few ambulatory patients who were not at the backgammon tourney crowded into the Common Room. Krebs wasn't quite sure how to handle it: on the one hand you didn't want to rush the body away like it was something obscene; on the other hand it seemed rather rude to leave the pajama-clad body on the cold floor. He had Wally lift Fred onto the nearer of the two white couches that faced each other across the burl table in front of the fireplace, and when Wendy arrived with his stethoscope he perched beside the body on the edge of the couch and listened formally but sincerely for a heartbeat. Then, in a gentle voice with just the right touch of gravity, he pronounced Fred Small officially dead at 10:05 P.M. The others had drawn around the couch in a loose circle. He turned to them, his reddish eyebrows arched behind the rose-rimmed spectacles. "I have the feeling I should give some kind of speech here. 'Win one for the Gipper' or something. All I can think of is to ask Wally to take Fred back to his cabin now. Emilia, would you like to help us prepare your father's body before we bring him down to the Viewing Room?"

Emilia looked wildly at Anne, who asked her if she'd rather come help put Danny to bed. She nodded gratefully. "But I'm not *tired*," Danny whined, and the classic lament made the grown-ups smile weakly. At any rate it settled some of the weird adrenal energy still flickering around the room: they were, after all, still survivors. All still survivors. Tom followed Wally's broad white back up the lighted path between the trees; Krebs stayed behind in the Common Room with the rest of his patients—he planned to brew up some Red Zinger and see who needed to talk.

———

The first step in Danny's M.I. was to go to his safe place. Krebs had started Danny out on a beach—*everybody* had a beach in his or her psyche—but as soon as the boy got the hang of it he chose his own safe place, which was, of course, the meadow that saddled the ridge east of the sun and west of the moon. Four times a day—before breakfast, after lunch, before supper, in bed before sleep—he would "visit" his safe place, relax, visualize the big dumb weak cancer cells and the busy white cells that wouldn't take no for an answer, and he'd try to think about his goal—you were supposed to set a goal—but no matter how many times Krebs explained it, when the time came, Danny would think about booting the kickball across the white line in the schoolyard. Right past that snotty little girl who used to tease him back when he first got sick and couldn't catch the ball anymore. Goal!

That was all, except that he was supposed to hang around in his safe place for a while and see if anybody appeared. If anybody did, that would be his Guide. This last was a touchy point for some thanatologists. The extreme left wing, spiritually speaking, thought the Guide figures were, for want of a better word, supernatural—the spirits of the great healers of the ages, perhaps, or arch- or sub-angels, hovering on some nearby astral plane, accessible to any mortal who believed in them. The right wing thought the Guides were just another phase of the visualization process and the patient analogous to a novelist who must believe his characters are alive and internally motivated. The Jungians found themselves, unfamiliarly enough, in the middle of the spectrum. It was all academic to Danny, who had yet to encounter his Guide, and was not at all sure he wanted any Spirits gliding around *his* meadow, anyway.

But the saddle ridge felt different the night Fred died. At first he couldn't get there. His mother sat at his bedside and guided him through the steps; Emilia sat at the edge of the sleeping loft, feet hanging down, but it wasn't her presence that bothered him. It was just that when he closed his eyes he saw Fred's face with its open eyes, and then he thought that behind their eyelids *everybody's* eyes were *always* open and staring, and that was an unsettling thought. So he pulled his soft blue blankie up to his chin and just *pretended* to imagine to be in his safe place, and soon he really *was* imagining it, and his mother's voice was farther and farther away. And the sky was purple and the sun a violent yellow abstract of a sun, sharp-pointed as a Sheriff's star over the purple ocean. And he knew he was not alone in the meadow.

Emilia was gone when Danny awoke; he could hear his mother and Tom Straw giggling up in the loft, and smell the pot smoke. He was of two minds about pot: he liked it when it made his mother young and silly and she would get right down on the floor and play; he hated it when she got quiet and far away from him. But tonight something in the way he felt when he woke up from his meadow-dream after meeting his Guide made the grown-ups' presence a little sad, for it was *he* who felt far away from *them*. Not frightened anymore. But tired and sad.

28

On the morning of the 26th of August, Danny announced to Tom Straw that Pengeena, who'd been the head honcho stuffed penguin since the dawn of the stuffed penguin era, was dead. "I see," said Tom. "You sure?" Seemed like it would be hard to tell with a stuffed penguin.

"Flat line."

"Dead enough," Tom agreed, and after bathing Danny, he dressed the boy in clean jeans, red socks and sneakers and a rugby shirt with broad maroon and yellow bands, and took him on an early morning search for a casket. First they dropped by the kitchen, where Dave, forearms and beard still dusted with flour from his pre-dawn baking, was unable to help them, but referred them to Vera, the no-nonsense Head Housekeeper, whom Dave referred to as the House Headkeeper. But Vera had a soft spot for Danny, as did the rest of her staff; she brought him an old shoebox from her own cabin. It fit Pengeena as snugly as if it had been built for her, and with a bandage scissors Tom cut away half the box top so the remains could be viewed.

Danny spent the morning taking Pengeena on a solemn tour of the hospice, and any of the grown-ups who felt inclined to laugh at the stuffed penguin in the Enna Jetticks coffin were dissuaded by the boy's dignity. "You were a good penguin," Krebs informed the little black-and-white corpse at breakfast. "And we'll miss you and think of you often." Danny, with the box in his lap, nodded seriously, as if glad to hear the departed get her due at long last, and with his left hand tapping delicately at the controls of the wheelchair set off up the trail. His hair had grown in fair; it was the color of oatmeal, and so wispy it puffed up like dandelion fluff even in the still air of the redwood grove.

The boy visited each of the cabins and suites in turn. He, too, had learned to call them by their Yankee names, because it would feel bad to think of *Fred's* cabin or *Sally's* cabin and then remember it wasn't their cabin anymore—that someone new was there who hadn't even known them, just like he didn't know anything about whoever had his room before him. He did not think about someone having his room after him. He bore the box on his lap from Yogi Berra to Moose Skowron to Hank Bauer, and so on. To the people he did not know well he would call from the door, or the porch, that "Pengeena my penguin died" and see if they wanted to invite him in. To his friends he would say only, "Pengeena died" and give them a moment to adjust before rolling up to show them the body. "You can pick her up," he would say. "She'd like that."

No doubt about it, the little coffin alone was enough to give Anne the creeps. And the way Danny was humorlessly carrying through this self-imposed ritual—the others might think it was cute, but it was all she could do not to scream at them all that *Goddammit, stuffed penguins can't die, too.*

The half-covered box haunted the corner of her vision all through Danny's post-lunch M.I.—he had his arm around it as if it were a teddy bear. She was relieved when he said he didn't need her to lead him through his session anymore, and turned the sling chair away from the bed so she wouldn't have to stare at the box. She thought about chucking the box, stiff stuffie and all, while he napped, but rejected it as something her mother would have done to her (which may have been the reason she thought of it in the first place).

She hoped he'd have forgotten about it when he woke from his nap, but if anything he was more earnest than ever. He brought Pengeena down to the Viewing Room off the Common Room downstairs and barely had enough strength and dexterity in his left hand to remove her from the box and lay her out on the bed, propped up rigidly against the pillows at a forty-five degree angle.

It was quiet inside the Viewing Room, which had been converted from a walk-in meat locker. It had blond panelling, an acoustic-tiled ceiling, several folding chairs, and a simple anonymous-looking bed covered with a cream and crimson Navajo blanket with a lightning-bolt design. Danny sat with his penguin for an hour. They only had one visitor—Wally—but then only Wally had been invited to the Viewing. That was because they—Danny and Pengeena—were going to need some help with the burial: there were secret plans afoot, and of all the grown-ups only Wally could be trusted with secret plans.

The funeral itself took place up in the vegetable garden at suppertime, which was Wally's only large block of free time that day. Only he and Danny attended the interment, and no words were spoken over the box, which had been wrapped around and around with masking tape until it was entirely sealed. And no sooner had the first spadeful of dirt thudded hollowly over the lid, then Danny lost interest in the proceedings entirely and rolled off to the fence dividing garden from pasture to visit Thalia.

Wally smoothed the dirt over the hole and walked away, leaving neither cross nor headstone, not so much as a toothpick to mark the grave. He watched Thalia nuzzling Danny through the rails and wished he could take the boy for a ride. It was such a delicious time of day: the broken earth of the garden still radiated the sun's warmth but the air held the cool blue promise of evening. Danny was so thin by now, though, and his muscle tone so poor that horseback would bruise him up too badly, no matter how Wally tried to cushion him with his own body. He carried the spade back to the toolshed and returned with a handful of oats for Danny to feed to the horse. But when he tried to feed her the grain trickled right through his fingers. Thalia didn't mind—she ate it off the ground and nuzzled his cheek for more.

———

Tom Straw, sleeping lightly as always in the loft that night, heard the door to the Mantle Suite open. He checked Little Ben with one eye—one o'clock—and sat up, his head just missing the ceiling, in time to see a white-clad figure creep across the room to stand for a moment by Danny's bed, lean down to tuck something under the child's pale blanket, and tiptoe out again, shutting the door quietly. *It's either Wally or the ghost of Hoss Cartwright,* thought Tom, and he lay back down.

———

Anne was awake by the time Tom finished dressing Danny the next morning, but could not drag herself out of the nesty warmth of the sleeping loft until some time later. Danny lay propped up on his pillows reading *The Velveteen Rabbit*, a familiar-looking penguin nestling in the crook of his right arm, her head peeking out from the sling. "Oh my God, Pengeena!" Anne's world slipped for a moment, as if a corpse had come to life. She recovered almost immediately, feeling ridiculous, but also a little giddy from the shock.

"It's not Pengeena," said Danny, but slyly, as if laying a trap.

"It's not?" Anne knew which penguin was which—hell, she could even tell the twins apart, and *they'd* both been plucked from the same bin at Toys R Us. She lowered the bars and sat on the edge of the bed.

"No, it's Shalala."

"Oh, and how did that work out?"

"Well, because, you know. . . . Well, Doc says when you die it just means you don't need your body anymore. That's how come they can do *transplants*, 'cause you're not *in* your body anymore so they can use pieces. Only with stuffies you can use the whole body."

"Krebs said all that?"

"Not Krebs. *Doc.*"

"Who's *Doc?*"

Danny thought for a moment, and looked away. He was clearly not comfortable with the question. "The man who comes to the meadow," he mumbled eventually.

"What meadow? Your safe place?"

He nodded reluctantly, and it was not until later, in the shower, with the hot water driving and the hot steam rising, that Anne understood that Danny's Guide, rather than helping in his cure, was instead helping him to come to terms with his own death. And she thought, as the tears began, of all those dumb old songs about crying in the rain so nobody would see your tears. *Why aren't there any songs about crying in the shower?*

But the tears came more easily by now, and were more easily washed away. "Hey, Slick," she called through the door after her shower. "Just what did you and Wally bury last night?"

"Only Vera's dumb old box," Danny replied. "Kch kch kch." And even with the door closed, Anne knew that he was cackling behind his hand like Ernie the Muppet from Sesame Street.

29

By September Danny was too weak to handle his wheelchair, so they set him up with an old-fashioned wooden-slatted invalid chair in which, propped by pillows, he could recline like a pasha on the patio, warmed by the sun and cooled by the redwood-scented breeze. There he'd daydream the afternoon away, weaving into archetypal images the events and imaginings of his life. *Once upon a time in a golden meadow east of the sun and west of the moon, a boy named Danny rode all by himself on his horse named Thalia, and she ran so hard her hooves made sparks, and she leaped like the cow-jumped-over-the-moon and flew through the blue sky, and weren't the birds surprised. They never saw a horse fly.* He would feel the joy of flying in his windpipe and his heart and be surprised to open his eyes and find himself in the invalid chair.

There was another dream-tale that came to him when he closed his eyes, that he somehow connected to *Doc,* as if *Doc* had told it to him once, someplace deep inside a dream. It was about his rescue from Protestant Mercy, only it wasn't really Protestant Mercy—for one thing, there were no children, and all the good people had turned into vampires and lady vampires. *Poor Danny, boy was he scared until his Mommy and Tom Straw rescued him.* But just like fairytales there was a sad part to the adventure: to be safe from the vampires, Danny and his mother and Tom Straw had to escape to Dr. Krebs's mountain, and they couldn't tell anyone where they'd gone. Not even Danny's Daddy, who sat behind a glass desk in a glass office high in the sky above San Francisco, and who was very rich and missed Danny very much.

He found himself thinking about his father often, but never more than on Labor Day weekend, when so many visitors came to the hospice. He'd even asked his mother on Sunday night whether she thought his father might come up for the Labor Day picnic the next day.

"He doesn't even know we're here," she said.

"But if he did know, would he come?"

"Yes, but he'd probably bring police to take you back to Protestant Mercy. You wouldn't want that, would you?"

Danny thought of the vampires, and shivered. "I guess not."

———

Anne asked Krebs about it the next morning. The two of them had hiked up to the meadow to set up a volleyball net for the picnic. "Why on earth is he getting so obsessed with his father. He hardly even *knows* him."

"Maybe that's why." Krebs drove the post-hole digger through the golden grass and turned up a few dry clods of earth.

"What do you mean by *that?*" Anne grabbed the pole in both hands, drove it into the hole, spread her legs for balance, closed her eyes, and felt the pole shudder when Krebs swung the sledgehammer.

He paused after a few swings. "Anne, I've seen an eighty-year-old man crying on his deathbed 'cause he never got straight with his father. There just seems to be a need sometimes. That's all I meant."

When the poles were sunk and guyed and the net strung, Anne and Krebs paced off a horseshoe pitch and drove the stakes for that, fed Thalia her morning oats and let her out of the little stable that sheltered her from the bobcats at night. Then Krebs returned to the hospice for rounds while Anne mucked out the stall.

She took her time strolling back to the compound—there was something soothing about the redwood grove, and the loamy path bordered with sword ferns and deer brush and squaw mat—and found Danny on the patio, reclining in his invalid chair. Visitors had already begun to arrive, and he had decided to show them how to lay out the potluck. "Wally and I figured it out," he told her proudly, pointing to the long folding tables set up in the shade, in the ell where the kitchen wing extended out from the back of the lodge. "Green salads, white salads, main foods. And we saved a whole table for dessert."

"Does this mean you might do us the honor of *eating* something for a change?" He had been off his feed for weeks and had grown quite thin.

"I tasted some sweet-potato pie. It was good, but I wasn't very hungry."

"How about if we put a piece in the refrigerator for later?"

"Okay. Could you save a piece for Marylou, too? She's probably too sick to come down."

"Sure. We could even bring it up to her if you want."

"Okay. But we need to check my leg bag first—I think it might be full."

She reached down to squeeze the bag. "No, not yet. How are you doing with the catheter, anyway. Does it hurt?"

"No, I don't even feel it. And I kind of like not having to think about peeing, or being afraid I'll mess up some more."

Anne rolled the creaking wooden chair up the shady path lined with lavendar impatiens and around to the back of the Whitey Ford cabin. Danny had the paper plate balanced on his lap, and she was encouraged to see him neaten up the edges of the whipped cream topping with his forefinger and suck the finger clean several times. He called out to Marylou when they reached the open door of the cabin.

"We're out here!" Marylou's daughter Samantha answered from the porch, and Anne rolled Danny through the wide, sillless doorway. The air was dry and cool in the cabin, the light a subdued umber; the porch was out back, enclosed by a redwood railing.

"You caught me getting my morning exercise," said Marylou, who was thirty-three years old, pale but otherwise not particularly unhealthy looking. She wore a bright orange kerchief on her head—she had been bald so long that she was even bald in her dreams—but would not wear a wig. ("I think it's gone beyond pretending," she would say, "much less fooling anybody.")

"Go right ahead, didn't mean to interrupt."

"No, this *is* my exercise. Trying not to crumple up—crumple down, I guess—in the wheelchair."

"Tom calls her Grandfather Smallweed," Samantha said, "after this character in a book he read, who's always sliding down in his chair so that they have to plump him up like a pillow." She was fifteen, soft-voiced and self-conscious.

"Bleak House, it's from *Bleak House."* Anne parked Danny's chair next to Marylou's and unfolded a green and white plastic-webbed chair for herself, after inspecting it for snails. "He calls Danny that, too, sometimes." Samantha took the pie from Danny and carried it inside. Anne sat facing downhill toward the lodge; she could see a white slice of patio through the trees.

"Uh-oh, look out, bird," warned Danny, pointing across the hill to the roof of a cabin below theirs, where Catsworth Osborne, Jr., the hospice cat, was creeping on his fat tortoiseshell belly toward a Townsend's Warbler on an overhanging branch.

"Don't worry," said Marylou. "Krebs said old Junior hasn't caught anything that moves faster than a bowl of Friskies in years." As she said it, the cat pounced, and the bird took to the air, crying *weasel weasel weasel.*

"Did you finish your letters?" Anne asked her. The dying woman had spent the last week saying good-bye to absent friends.

"Yes, yes I did. The last twenty or so were pretty much the same letter, though. Samantha rode into Miller Bay with Wally and Xeroxed it, then I just wrote a little something personal on each one. Want to hear it?"

"Sure."

Marylou closed her eyes and recited from memory. " 'Dear . . . whoever.

" 'As you know, two years ago I was diagnosed as having leukemia. Since then I've tried every form of treatment from chemotherapy to witchcraft, and I'm grateful for everything that was there for me to try. But the time for that is over now, and the time left is for saying good-bye.

" 'I'm not *happy* about it, mind you—I'll be sorry to leave you all—but I'm grateful I had her early enough and lived long enough to see my daughter Samantha grow up to be such a beautiful and kind young woman.' "

"Ma-om," Samantha moaned, still embarrassed though she had typed the letter herself.

"Well, you are," said Marylou; she and Anne exchanged

knowing parental smiles. "Then I just told them how nice it is up here, and that they were welcome to come up and visit—not to worry because I still look pretty much the way I always did—but if they want to see me they'd better make it soon. It was easier than I thought it would be."

She was visibly tired. Anne offered to help her back to bed while Samantha took Danny back down to the patio.

"Maybe give me five more minutes," Marylou replied. "But Sam, you go ahead and take Danny. You've been stuck up here all morning."

That was fine with Danny, who had a puppy-love crush on the teenager with the long blond hair. "I'm lucky I'm not going to have to say good-bye to *my* Mom," the two mothers overheard him telling Samantha as she rolled him through the cabin.

"Oh?"

"No, 'cause my Mom and me, we don't say good-bye. We say, 'See you later, alligator.' "

———

Danny spent the next hour or so out on the patio, sipping honey lemonade through a straw while Samantha massaged his scalp with coconut oil, fed him tidbits from the potluck, and combed his hair over and over again. He was in heaven—he had her hold up a mirror so he could see himself. "I've got eyebrows too, now, you know," he said, as she rolled him into the shade for his nap.

Visitors and volunteers continued to arrive throughout the afternoon, bearing casseroles, leftovers from other Labor Day gatherings, even a huge crock of homemade vanilla ice cream, and as the shadows lengthened a red-eyed, pony-tailed Hurok Indian named Frank, whose mother had been cared for at the hospice the previous winter, arrived with a freshly netted salmon the size of a small pig, lying in state in a washtub full of ice in the back of a bright new Mazda pickup.

Danny begged to be allowed to stay up until the salmon was cooked—he hated fish only a little less than he hated going to bed in the middle of a party—but he could barely keep his eyes open as Tom and Anne wheeled him to their room, where together they performed the little caring rituals that were a part of their life together: bedpan, sponge bath, floss and brush, vital signs, catheter, M.I. Then Tom kissed him goodnight and returned to the party to become one of too many cooks supervising the salmon.

Anne pulled the sling chair up close to the bed and sat with her boy until Wally came to relieve her. They were keeping a watch over him because he rarely slept through the night anymore, and didn't like being alone. On the other hand, he didn't mind waking up so often if it meant seeing his mother's face, or Tom Straw with his miniature reading light clamped to a fat orange-spined book, or Wally with his guitar in his lap and his Folksinger's Wordbook propped open against the side of Danny's leg.

Danny rarely tired of hearing Wally sing "The Frozen Logger," or "The Cat Came Back," or of singing along with the macabre chorus of "The Titanic," but it was not until Wally held the book up and turned the pages for Danny that the boy discovered the song with his own name in the title. He had Wally sing "Danny Boy" twice over, and thereafter asked for it every night, until by mid-September Anne blanched at the first breath of the Londonderry Air. Wally even tried leaving out the third verse for her once, the one that went: "And if you come when all the flowers are dying/ And I am dead as dead I well may be/ You'll come and find the place where I am lying/ And kneel and say an Ave there for me."

They thought they'd gotten away with it, too, until Wally's next visit. "Anything you want to hear, Danny?"

"Yeah. 'Danny Boy.' The *whole song.*"

In his heart Wally agreed with the boy: though he could see why it would be painful for Anne, to Wally it was worth going through that third verse so that the fourth made sense: "And I shall hear, tho' soft you tread above me/ And all my dreams will warm and sweeter be/ If you will not fail to tell me that you love me/ I'll sleep in peace until you come to me."

The first time Tom overheard the performance was the Sunday evening following Labor Day. He and Krebs were up in the loft playing backgammon. Their eyes met over the board.

"As Oscar Wilde once remarked," said Straw, " 'It takes a heart of stone to read the death of Little Nell without laughing.' "

Krebs smiled, glad for the joke, for it was ten o'clock, and Marylou had died shortly before eight.

30

The middle of September was always a busy time at the hospice: to prepare for the rainy Bigfoot County winter they brought the patients in from the farthest cabins to the nearer ones and to the rooms in the lodge, put up the green awnings over the patio and the paths between the nearer cabins and the lodge, cleared out the culverts and the drains under the road that led to the county road—that sort of thing. Krebs was always a little short of money by September, so they all pitched in.

Anne volunteered for the rooftop work. She found she liked scrambling around up there in the sweet thin air clearing fallen needles and old nests from the aluminum gutters and downspouts, cutting back overhanging redwood boughs that might scrape the shingles in a storm, and in general outraging the bushy-tailed red squirrel population. "I know you," she told them. "You're just rats in drag." She worked in jeans and a hooded sweatshirt; her faded red Nikes felt sure and nimble on the dark shingles. She found herself smiling at the Steller's jay scolding *shook shook shook* in the sunlight slanting through the dark green air and wondered how long they had before the rains came. Another month, month-and-a-half, tops. All over Bigfoot County pot growers had one eye on their crops and the other on the sky for the government helicopters and camera planes with banded wings, as well as for the first rains. They too were preparing for autumn, setting up drying sheds and hiring guards and harvesters and lining up trimmers. A good trimmer could clear a hundred a day, cash money, tax-free. It had occurred to Anne that she might stay on up in Bigfoot after . . . after. . . .

It scared her a little that she could not say "after Danny dies," even to herself—that was like poor Bea. Still the thoughts that haunted her most were not those of death, but of life: what would it be like, trying to go to sleep the first night, *after* . . . ? Or waking up, the first morning? What if she felt free? Free as here on the roof, free of everything but gravity. Then what would Danny's life have meant?

She shook herself and stretched like a cat waking from a nap, way up on her tiptoes on the peak of Yogi Berra's roof. The best part about being up there was what you *didn't* have to think about.

———

Danny opened his eyes. "Tom?" he said—he seemed surprised. "I dreamed."

"Nice dream?"

"Sea otters." As he had seen them two years ago, floating on their backs in the icy green water off Point Lobos, squinting at the sun like funny cartoon beavers.

"Yeah, they're neat." Tom marked his page and put the book down. "What can I get you? You thirsty? How about a massage?"

"Could I have a mustard?"

"Say what?"

Danny looked puzzled. "Not a mustard."

"I didn't think so. I think you said a different word than you meant. That happens sometimes."

"Yeah." But the boy's eyes were skittish.

"Bet it felt really weird, hunh? And you know what, I bet the harder you try to say the word you mean, the harder it'll be."

"How did you know that?"

"The Shadow Knows. Nyahaha! C'mon, let's play Twenty Questions for it. You know how to play Twenty Questions?" Danny nodded. "Okay, bet you I get it in five. Is it bigger than a breadbox?"

"You're supposed to say animalvegebalormineral." But Danny felt better already—*good old Tom Straw.* He got his sip of orange juice and closed his eyes and for some reason found himself thinking about Halloween, about all the Halloweens he could remember. When he was three his red plastic devil's mask kept slipping down over his eyes, and when he was four it rained and Mommy made him wear a raincoat over his costume, and last year was the best because they had a party at Adam's and a whole bunch of kids went trick-or-treating together and because they were all almost five the Mommies had to walk way behind.

Danny fell asleep thinking about Halloween, and when he opened his eyes again Tom Straw was still there. "Let me see your penguin," the boy asked; Tom Straw held his paperback up close and turned the little light so Danny could see the oval Penguin logo on the spine. Then he dipped the book so Shalala could see it. Tom kissed Danny on the forehead before he leaned back, and the boy felt a spasm of love for the comfortable bony man whose name was Straw, whose hair was straw. "Louie?" said the child.

"What?" Tom's lips formed the word, but he could not speak: he knew what was coming.

"I think this is the beginning of a beautiful friendship."

———

On the day of the Autumnal Equinox it was decided at the staff meeting that Danny, like the sun, had crossed an imaginary line, and for the first time they charted his condition as Rapid Decline (Active Dying, Slow Decline, Level, and Improving were the other classifications). After the meeting Wendy Wane ferried two patients into Miller Bay for palliative radiation sessions and returned that afternoon with some disturbing news: the hospital there had received a flyer early in August (apparently from a computer-generated mass mailing) describing Danny, Tom, and Anne, with a San Francisco number to call if the boy were brought in for treatment. It was not until two weeks after the Labor Day picnic that one of the nurses chanced upon the notice on an out-of-the-way bulletin board and connected the little boy at Krebs's with the flyer.

"Wanted Dead or Alive," said Tom, when Wendy pulled him aside at lunch to tell him. "I hope you told her it was just a coincidence."

"Sure," said the chubby blond nurse. "I told her it was some *other* kid named Danny and some *other* six-foot-eight one-legged male nurse named Tom Straw."

"Great. Thanks." They were standing in the kitchen doorway, Tom stooping slightly. They parted at Dave's "Hot stuff comin' through"—he passed between them with a steaming pot of rice and beans—and they moved into the kitchen.

"Look, it's going to be okay," she whispered. "Tania took the flyer down—she doesn't think anybody else who was up here saw it. And she sure won't turn a kid in, at least not to his father—she hates men."

"Oh well, *that's* reassuring. Did she happen to remember the number? I'm curious whether it was Pierce's office or the cops or what?"

"I don't know. I'll try to find out." She had perched on a butcher block table; Dave returned and scolded her: "I chop food where you have parked your ass, m'dear."

"No, never mind, don't call her," said Tom, when the cook was out of earshot. "I don't even *want* to know."

Tom waited until he and Anne were alone in bed that night to tell her. She wasn't surprised. "I never thought for a minute Pierce would give up. I'm only sorry I let you get mixed up in this."

"No, we're in it together," he insisted, and she wondered, not for the first time, whether they would be together . . . *after.*

———

One morning early in October Dave provoked the jays to a feeding frenzy with the burnt pan-scrapings of the breakfast walnut-carrot loaf. The thin autumn sunlight had not yet warmed the redwood grove; in the undergrowth the bright red huckleberries and the yellow buttons of the pearly everlasting were further signs of the subtle change of season, and when Wally climbed the hill to feed Thalia it seemed to him her coat had begun to darken for winter. He dumped the #10 can of oats in the trough, and when she had eaten he slipped a rope halter on her and led her down the path toward the cabins and the lodge. The clip-clop of her shod hooves on the asphalt turned heads all over the grounds. He tied her to the redwood nearest the patio and hurried inside.

Fifteen minutes later the elevator doors slid open on the ground floor of the lodge and Wally emerged pushing a gurney piled high with blankets through the Common Room, out the glass doors and across the patio, with Anne close behind him.

Tom and Krebs, watching the curious procession from the porch of the Arts and Crafts cabin, deduced that Danny was underneath all those blankets long before his pallid face peeked out. They watched Wally untie Thalia and lead her over, saw her nuzzling the blankets and heard the child laughing. Krebs turned to Tom—behind his rose-rimmed glasses his eyes were suspiciously moist—and shook his finger in the taller man's face. "If you so much as *mention* Oscar Wilde," he joked, "I'll see to it you never work in this town again."

Chapter

31

On a rainy night in mid-October Krebs lit a fire in the Common Room and settled down to a game of Monopoly, Bigfoot County style—two *thousand* dollars for passing Go, but *nobody* gets out of jail free—with Tom Straw, Anne, and Wendy. Wally was with Danny in Mickey Mantle, and Leah with Mr. Mars in the Skowron Suite across the way. Only those two were classified as Active Dying, although in Danny's case Krebs was no longer sure: Active Dying generally lasted one to five days, but Danny was still hanging on after two weeks.

Krebs was an excellent Monopoly player. He'd done it once in real life: it was only with the rents he'd receive in October or November from pot growers on property he owned either directly or through Illinois Blind Trusts that he was able to keep the hospice afloat without booting patients out when they'd outlived their coverage. He was all too aware that this was a luxury few hospices enjoyed. In the rest of the country it was best, if you were poor, to die within your allotted time.

Tonight it seemed Krebs couldn't keep his mind on the game: he bankrupted early, sold the remainder of his holdings to Wendy for a kiss, and went off to wander the battlements alone. Out back the patio awning had been rolled up for the night; he looked up past the frame to the dark underside of the redwoods and the lighter patches of sky peeking through. Soft filtered rain dripped steadily on the patio and puddled up in the depression in the middle where the form had buckled when they were pouring the concrete. The cabins were all dark, squatting stolidly on the hill, their shake shingles shrugging off the rain. *Ten o'clock and all's well,* Krebs thought. Only something wasn't well. He walked around the side of the lodge and in through the side entrance, leaving his wet boots just inside the screen door, padding through the dark pantry in thick-heeled socks; in the night kitchen the pots and pans hung from the ceiling like bats.

Krebs heard the laughter of the Monopolists on his way upstairs; he opened the door of the Skowron room without knocking and Leah turned around to give him the okay sign with thumb and forefinger. Her long hair was crow black in the yellow glow of the reading lamp; Mr. Mars lay on his back, peacefully asleep, whistling softly through the winking tracheotomy hole in his throat. Krebs shut the door quietly and tiptoed down the hall to his own room, where he retrieved a Stride-Rite shoebox from the back of his closet. Then he circled the gallery until he came to Danny's open door. "How's it going, Wal'?"

The orderly put his guitar down and crossed the room silently on rubber-soled white canvas shoes that Danny had once said looked like they'd fit Babar. "I don't know, Dr. K. I just don't know. An hour ago I was halfway to the door to call you guys in. Now he's . . . take a look."

Krebs crossed to the bedside, checked the boy swiftly with his practiced eye, pulled back the covers to watch the emaciated chest rise, flutter, fall. "I see." He straightened an imaginary crimp in the sheepskin and covered the boy again. "Look, Wally, I want to take over for you here. You can knock off if you want—just tell Tom and Anne I need some time with Danny. I'll call them when I'm done."

Wally picked up his guitar by the neck. "Sure you don't want me to stick around?"

Krebs shook his head. "Just want to have a little talk with my patient. Man to man."

"What's in the box?"

"Magic, my friend. Magic."

———

"Danny? It's Dr. Krebs." He lowered the side bar, drew back the covers, and lifted Danny in his arms, careful not to foul the catheter tubing as he sat down in the sling chair with the boy in his lap. "You going to wake up for me, son? Got some nifty stuff to show you." He lifted the boy vertically and hugged him to his chest as if he were going to burp him. With one hand he supported the back of Danny's head and with the other draped the boy's arms over his shoulders as if Danny were hugging him, and rocked the boy gently back and forth until he heard a break in the slow rhythmic breathing pattern. When he lowered Danny to his lap again, the child was watching him with those solemn hazel eyes. Dark green flecked with gold. Like the redwood grove in the morning sunshine. "Pitter-patter," said the boy.

"What?" Then Krebs heard the rain on the roof. "Oh yeah. Nice sound, hunh?"

"Nice." Danny's head rested in the crook of Krebs's elbow. With his other hand Krebs showed him the shoebox. "What's in it?"

"C'mon, let's get you back into bed and I'll show you." Krebs lay Danny back down and cranked the boy up to a sitting position, propped with pillows on either side. He watched Danny's eyelids fighting to close and made a big show of opening the box as he pulled the chair up to the head of the bed. "Now there are three things in here," said Krebs, adjusting the box primly on his lap. He had good calm hands. "And even if you were big and strong as Wally I wouldn't show 'em to you all at once—too much of a shock to your system." He winked. "By the way, how you feeling? Can I get you anything?"

"Nunh-unh." Danny kept his eyes on the box. Krebs pierced the brittle yellow scotch-tape seal with his thumbnail and slit it open on three sides. He started to flip the top back, then pretended to notice Danny staring. He smiled coyly and turned his back. "S'okay? S'okay. S'aright? S'aright." He flipped the box open and shut and his reddish eyebrows wiggled as he gave the boy a minute of vintage Senor Wences. Danny laughed for the first time that day and started to say something, but forgot.

"I know, I know," said Krebs. "What's in the box? Okay, numero uno . . ."

Eighteen baseball cards. Not just any baseball cards: these were of the Yankees whose names graced the cabins and suites of the hospice. They were brown-spotted with mildew and the gray cardboard was soft with age, fanning apart at the corners, but the faces were recognizable: Moose Skowron with his Frankenstein brow, Mantle's boyish smile and Bauer's scowl, old Yogi homely as a fig. . . . One by one Krebs held them up for Danny, then replaced them in the box.

"What else?" asked the boy, but it was a Christmas morning "what else?" and Krebs smiled.

"Not so fast, my boy—you'll get the bends. Now close your eyes." He placed the box on the floor and with the pads of his thumbs gently massaged Danny's eyesockets all the way around. "You like that?"

"Really. Makes me see colored lights . . . like fireworks."

"Did you get to see any fireworks this year, or were you in the hospital?"

"Saw 'em. On the roof. That was the night Toni died."

Krebs's thumbs never stopped moving. When he'd finished the eyesockets he moved up to the forehead, rubbing from the third eye out over the eyebrows to the temples. "Were you there?"

"Unh-hunh."

"What was it like?"

"Okay. But then the next day Bea killed herself. Everybody got mad at her."

"Why did she do that?"

"She would be too lonesome to live without Toni. Is it time for the box?"

"I suppose. Okay, numero two-o . . ." He picked up the box and pulled out an electroplated locket with a cameo on the lid of a woman's profile carved in relief from fake ivory. Krebs pressed the catch, and the lid clicked open. Danny looked in. "Dirt?" he said dubiously.

"From the pitcher's mound at Yankee Stadium. And the best part is"—Krebs licked his thumb and rubbed it in the locket, then smeared a dab of mud on the tip of Danny's nose— "when your mother asks how you managed to get your face dirty just lying in bed, you can tell her the dirt is from . . ."

"Yankee Stadium."

"Blow her mind. Boom!"

"Boom!"

The doctor snapped the locket shut and replaced it in the box. He picked up Shalala the penguin, formerly Pengeena, from the floor and propped her on Danny's shoulder. He began massaging *her* fuzzy head. "How's that feel?" he asked her.

"Good," said Danny in his squeaky penguin voice. He had closed his eyes.

Thank you, thought Krebs—they had stumbled into play therapy. "I never massaged a penguin before. What's your name?"

"Pengeena."

Oh really? This was getting interesting. "Why, Pengeena, I thought you died?"

"I did." Danny's eyes were still closed.

Krebs continued to massage the little stuffed head. "So I guess you know all about dying and stuff."

"The Shadow Knows. Nyahaha."

Bet he got that from Straw. Krebs kept his eyes on the stuffie; with Danny nearly motionless it was not hard for Krebs to maintain the willing suspension of disbelief so useful in play therapy. "So tell me, Pengeena, was it scary? Did it hurt?"

"Not really. There's nothing to be scared about. You just follow the light."

Krebs decided to push a little. "Does Danny know that?"

"Sure."

"So it's not like he's afraid to die?"

"Not him!"

That was emphatic enough. In Krebs's experience there were two reasons why human beings hung on as tenaciously as the boy in front of him: either they were afraid to die, or they had unfinished business. He remembered his Labor Day conversation with Anne. "Pengeena, is there somebody who would be too lonesome, like Bea, if Danny died?"

The penguin nodded. *No wait, goddammit, the penguin didn't nod. Jesus, you're losing it, Krebs.* But he sensed the "yes" just the same. "Who?"

"Ask Danny," said Danny in his penguin voice. So Krebs did. The boy opened his eyes. "What's the third thing in the box?" he asked, in his own voice, and Krebs wondered, not for the first time, just who the hell was in charge around here, anyway.

"Okay, numero three-o . . ." No flourishes this time. Krebs held up a baseball, horsehide darkened to antique ivory, and rotated it slowly in front of Danny's eyes until the signature came into view. Danny's lips formed the name: *Babe Ruth.* "Is it real?"

"My father got the autograph himself. He kept it in his dresser. Me and my brothers were only allowed to touch it every so often like on our birthdays, or for a reward. We chose for it after he died. Once-twice-three shoot." Krebs reenacted the historic moment. "I won." He cupped the boy's hands together in his lap and placed the ball between them. With only the bedside lamp on, the shadows were stark in the white-washed room. The fingers of Danny's left hand tried to grip the ball, but could barely conform to the sphere. The rain had stopped, but the redwoods still dripped musically and would for hours.

"Who was your daddy?" Danny asked.

"He was Dr. Krebs, too."

"What'd he die of?"

Krebs tapped the center of his chest. "Heart."

"Do you miss him?"

"Sometimes."

"Do you know my daddy?"

"No, we've never met."

"Well he's who."

"He's who what?"

"He's who . . . you know."

"He's who would miss you too much?"

Danny nodded; his left palm patted the ball weakly. "I know because when he came to see me one time at the Casa where we used to live, when I wasn't even as sick as I am now but I didn't hardly have any hair, he felt so bad when he saw me that he ran away." *Think of it*, said his wide eyes: *a grown man running away.* "It was my fault. I should of wore my Giants hat. And then we had to leave so they wouldn't do the treatment again. He doesn't even know my hair grew back."

"I see, said the blind carpenter," Krebs commented.

"An' he picked up his hammer and saw."

Krebs held Danny's hand until the boy fell asleep; when he packed the baseball back into the box and closed the top, there was in the gesture something of the pediatrician packing up his black bag after a successful housecall.

———

Tom Straw lay awake in the dark sleeping loft, thinking about his father and staring up at the white ceiling a few feet above his nose. Beside him, Anne slept uneasily. She'd started grinding her teeth in the past few weeks—sounded like bones crunching. He had been thinking about his old man off and on in the hours since Krebs had told him what he'd learned from Danny. John Straw had been a custodian in the Newark Public School System. Shot and beer man. Hands the size of a first baseman's mitt. He and Tom hadn't made peace with each other until the last few months of the old man's life. Tom had been stationed at St. Albans then—that's where he met Krebs—and he'd been able to spend much of his leave at his father's bedside. Nothing profound had happened—they watched tv and played gin; they never even came close to acknowledging the feeling that had grown between them—but now when Tom remembered his father he thought of a big-boned old man with mild blue eyes and wispy hair that had once been the color of straw, who laughed until his poor lungs hurt when Red Skelton did the seagulls, Gertrude and Heathcliff, who maintained a childlike delight in pro wrestling and roller derby, but thought Pa Cartwright was a smug asshole, and who (Tom's mother wrote him, in Nam) had the gilt-framed picture of Tom in his dress whites set up on the bedside table before he died. Right next to the John F. Kennedy memorial ashtray.

Tom Straw sat up; only his tall man's reflexive hunch kept him from banging his head on the ceiling. He rolled out of bed and hopped down the ladder one-legged, naked. He pulled on his stump sock, strapped on his leg and dressed in the dark, threw a clean black T-shirt and his best driving tapes, his sunglasses and raingear into his overnight bag, and limped to the door. He turned back, though, first to write Anne a note, then to kneel by Danny's bedside and whisper through the bars. "Danny, it's Tom. Can you hear me?" The child muttered something, probably in his sleep. *Close enough*, thought Tom. "Danny, I'm going down to San Francisco. I'm going to bring your daddy back with me."

Danny turned his head; their eyes met through the bars. "Promise?"

Tom thought it over for a second. "Yeah, what the hell," he

said; it occurred to him that that was exactly how his father would have phrased it, too. "See you later, alligator."

"After awhile, crocodile? . . ." replied Danny, on a rising inflection.

"Mañana, iguana? . . ." said Tom.

But Danny was ready. "Off to see the wizard, lizard," he said, and he smiled triumphantly.

32

Anne read Tom's note in the harsh white Tensor light, switched it off and burrowed down deeper under the covers. *I wash my hands* . . . she thought over and over. *I wash my hands.* . . . But she felt the courage of the last few weeks seeping away as she pictured Tom Straw in jail. He thought he was tough—he *was* tough—but Pierce was tough, too, and vengeful. And oh to have Danny die and Tom Straw not at her side. Not just alone, but *alone* alone. *Please God, that wouldn't be fair.* She climbed out of bed and took the top comforter—cornflowers on a wheat background—down the ladder with her, turned on the bedside lamp, sat in the sling chair, and pulled the comforter over her shoulders. She opened the book Tom had left on the bedside table. *David Copperfield.* She wriggled her shoulders and settled back in the chair. *"Chapter I. I am Born.* Whether I shall turn out to be the hero of my own life, or whether that station will be held by anybody else, these pages must show. . . ." Anne's eyes slid right off the page; she thought about Tom Straw out there on the highway. *Men,* she thought. *Heroes. Tom, we didn't need any heroes.* She forced her eyes back to the book.

———

It was a good night for driving. Green dashboard glow, white headlights streaming past on the left, red taillights falling back on the right, window down, tape deck up, and the smell of California after the rain: surely the Comet was born for such a night. Tom Straw stopped once for gas and a whizz, and once at a 7-11 for coffee in a cardboard cup the size of a bucket and a microwaved breakfast sandwich that contained no recognizably organic substance. He ate as he drove, and wondered as he ate whether he was being a damn fool. But when he thought about the possibility of Pierce having him thrown in jail, he thought as well of Danny and his unfinished business. Oh, the boy would die eventually, father or no father—willpower could do some pretty amazing things, but in the end either you made your peace or you didn't. The body can only struggle so long. But *how* long? Until the kid was blind? Blown up like a balloon? Tom Straw knew what Anne only suspected, what Krebs knew but would not say: willpower can keep a boy alive a terribly long time. No, the only question for Tom Straw was who was going to bell the cat?

So what could Tom Straw do, but hop in his Comet and ride. South. South is easy in California: just keep the ocean on your right and America on your left.

———

The next morning's storm drenched the coast from the Oregon border to San Luis Obispo. The first fat drops on the lodge roof raised Anne from her Copperfield trance. Secure in her certain knowledge that the shingles were sound and the gutters clear, she sang, "Rain on the Roof" to the sleeping boy, then bent her head to her book again. Wally, who had cancelled his day off to take Tom's patient load, dropped in to spell her for an early breakfast, but she would not leave Danny, so he brought her a bowl of oatmeal and raisins for breakfast. She ate one-handed, engrossed in her book; milk dribbled down her chin and onto the comforter. She dabbed at it with the bedside kleenex, but had routed so much of her anxiety into Copperfield's adventures that she would not put the book down, would not leave *his* side either, at least until he had reached safe harbor at Aunt Betsy's. Then, red-eyed, stiff-necked, with little crabs of pain digging at the small of her back, she threw off the comforter, rose and stretched, peed and showered, irrigated Danny's Foley, gave him a bedbath—he murmured but did not awaken— and made up the bed with him in it, rolling him on his side like an old pro. He opened his eyes briefly when she lifted him to put on a fresh pair of pj's—Leah had found him Dr. Dentons at a rummage sale at her daughter's school—but he only smiled at her and closed them again. She turned him on his side to take the pressure off his bony butt and heels where the tissue was beginning to break down, then settled back in the bedside chair with her book, drew her feet under her, and lowered herself into the fiction as if into a warm bath, half-submerged, tranquilized as well by the patter of the rain.

⸺

The last hours of the journey were slow torture. The storm had traffic on the Golden Gate Bridge backed up to the Waldo Grade, and the smug drive-time disc jockeys warned of everything but frogs and famine. Cops in shiny yellow slickers were turning back light cars and trucks with high profiles from the windy bridge and convoying the rest single file past the overturned hulk of a blue and yellow Chronicle truck. The low-riding Comet was waved on through. This struck Tom as yet another good news/bad news joke: he could hardly see the taillights of the car ahead, the span shivered alarmingly, and he wasn't exactly in a goddam hurry to get where he was going anyway.

⸺

Cindy Hardy, whose husband was in a Slow Decline two doors down in the Phil Rizzuto Suite, stopped by later that morning with a cup of tea for Anne, who looked up reluctantly from her book and only put it down when she saw that the other woman needed to talk. "Is that a good book?" Cindy asked.

It took Anne a moment to get a handle on the question. "Oh. Yeah . . . it's just . . . you get so deep into it it's like you forget it's a book." She'd nearly fallen through the Looking Glass.

"I wish *this* was all a book," said Cindy, gesturing to include Danny, the room, the hospice where her husband was dying, the sky above: the whole enchilada.

"I know," said Anne. They talked about the rain instead, and Dave's cooking and local politics, but after Cindy had gone Anne dredged up in excruciating detail a conversation she'd had with Tom back in June, shortly after they'd become lovers. It had been a slow night on tv, and she'd asked him to recommend a book. "You ever read *David Copperfield?*"

"Is that the one where the mother dies in childbirth at the beginning?"

"No, that's *Oliver Twist.* This is the one where she lives long enough to marry the wicked stepfather and *then* dies."

"Pass."

"No, but it's not like that, it's not depressing, 'cause you can always trust Dickens—it always comes out okay in the end. Guaranteed."

"I wish he was writing *this*, then." She'd gestured, just as Cindy had. "Then Danny would get better."

"Not necessarily," Tom had said off-handedly, and blithely embroidered a Dickens ending for her: "But if Dickens did have him die, he'd have you and me end up getting married and having a little boy that looked like me, poor bastard, and a little girl like you, and every Christmas they'd climb on our laps and we'd tell them the story about how we met and about Danny, and the little boy would say, 'How I wish Danny could be with us to share this Christmas,' and the girl would reach up and wipe a tear from your eye and say, 'Don't cry mother, for I'm quite sure that somehow Danny *is* here with us every Christmas, and so shall he always be so long as we remember him,' or something like that."

And Anne, who'd been in a tough-guy mood, had pretended to gag herself with her finger and throw up inside her shirtfront—"Bleagh!"

Now, in October, the remembered conversation struck Anne rather differently. She turned back to her book and tried to read it through her tears. " 'He's a-going out with the tide,' said Mr. Peggoty. 'People can't die along the coast except when the tide's pretty nigh out.' " And the hospice faded from Anne's consciousness until her tears were not for Danny or the Hardings or herself, but for dear old Peggoty, and for Barkis, as, it being low water, he went out with the tide.

33

The rain gusted in glassy sheets through the downtown canyons. Tom pulled his olive drab poncho tighter; the wind toyed with him like a tai-chi master—push-pull, push-pull—and sent him staggering once in a Ray Bolger Scarecrow dance. A sidewalk umbrella peddler caught his elbow and steadied him. "Hokay now?"

"Thanks, I got it."

"Humbrella? Three dollah?"

"You kidding? I'd take off like Mary Poppins." Not likely: the sidewalks were littered with the inside-out skeletons of three-dollar umbrellas, black skin flapping in patches from broken ribs.

The janitor had the Wet Floor signs and the buckets and mops out in the lobby of Pierce's building. Tom rode up alone in a dank elevator. The Pierce Felger and McCloskey waiting room was empty save for the receptionist behind a chrome and glass desk. "Hi," he said.

"Hi." She slipped her shoes on and put her magazine away while Tom hung his poncho on an angular chrome coatrack. She'd thought at first he was a messenger—he certainly looked ratty enough, with his sneakers squishing on the decorator gray carpet, jeans soaked black from the knees down, black T-shirt and Levi jacket with cut-off sleeves. "Can I help you?"

Tom knew he looked like hell, and smiled to reassure her. *"God,* I hope so." And he began the speech he'd been rehearsing for some two hundred miles.

———

Danny's breathing grew stertorous just before noon. He woke up while Krebs was examining him, though, and was able to clear his windpipe on his own. This was good, the doctor told Anne: he didn't want to have to use suction so late in the game. (Perhaps some hyoscine at the end to dry up the secretions so there'd be no death rattle.) He offered to spell her for a while, but she refused.

"Maybe after lunch?"

"Maybe." They did not mention Tom Straw.

———

The long table in the conference room was chrome and glass, the chairs chrome and cane. The receptionist brought Tom a cup of coffee and closed the door behind her. He wondered for a moment if she'd locked him in, and decided he'd rather not know. He thought about jail—city jail. Would he have to wear an orange jumpsuit? Would they have one his size? He wasn't afraid for himself physically—he had a quick fantasy of unstrapping his leg and swinging it like a club to keep the hordes of drag queens at arm's length—but the thought of breaking his promise to Danny turned his bowels weak. *Never should have promised.* But he knew why he had: so he couldn't quit, turn back. *It worked: no turning back now.* The door opened. Pierce, in shirt-sleeves. *He's got Danny's hazel eyes,* thought Tom. *Or vice-versa.*

———

People just seemed to gravitate toward the Mantle Suite as the afternoon wore on. Wally dropped in for a while when his shift was over (Krebs had by then sent for his backup nurse to cover for Tom); the grim old House Headkeeper Vera spent an hour at the bedside while Anne lay down in the loft to rest her back and her eyes; Krebs dragged the sling chair in from his suite and settled in for a long stay. It stopped raining around three; at four Dave brought up a tray of sandwiches and a thermos of tea. Anne smiled her thanks and went back to her book. Dora weakened; Emily was disgraced. Anne read on through her tears. Sometimes the only sounds in the room were Anne turning the pages and sniffling, and the occasional rattling snore from Krebs, who'd fallen asleep in his chair. Dora died. Her damn dog died. *Tom, if you lied . . . ,* thought Anne. *If there's no happy ending . . .* She read on.

———

The clock on the wall of the conference room at Pierce Felger & McCloskey was one of those understated modern jobs that only hinted discreetly at the time: not quite eleven-thirty when Pierce first walked in and said, "Well?" Meaning: your serve, Straw.

Tom spread his hands wide, weaponless. He thought of one of Frieda's not infrequent laments: *So many victims, so few villains.* "Roger," he said, "Danny's dying. He asked for you, he wants to see you."

Pierce kept his eyes on Tom, but only by force of will. "Jesus," he said. With forefinger and thumb he plucked the pack of Camel straights from the breast pocket of his white shirt, tapped one out for himself and offered the pack to Tom.

"No thanks, I gave . . . yeah, what the hell." The lawyer lit up—the civilized rasp of a Zippo—and handed the bronze lighter to Tom. *U.S.M.C.* was engraved on it. Tom fired up, took a handsome drag of the roasty toasty smoke, and frenched the end of the puff through his nostrils. "My brand," he said nostalgically. In the offer and acceptance of the cancer stick, things had changed: they were no longer stray dogs pissing on a beach, but men in council. Enemies, perhaps, but in council.

Pierce pocketed the lighter. "It's like he's dying twice. Because I already . . . I'd already given him up. Bruner said he wouldn't last six weeks without treatment. I papered every hospital in the country. I figured I'd never see him again."

"I can take you to him, but we have to leave soon—there's not much time."

"You know I can have you put away." It was not a question.

"You can do that later. This way you get to see your son."

———

No sunset that night, just a gradual silvering of the tough gray sky to the west. Danny opened his eyes a few minutes after six. "Where's that Tom Straw?" he asked playfully, the way his mother used to say, "Where's that Danny Dawson?" if it was dinnertime and he was pretend-hiding in his bed with his head under the covers like an ostrich; the way she said it would make him giggle and she would "find" him and swoop him off to the kitchen.

Anne swabbed at Danny's dry lips with a Q-tip dipped in lemon-flavored glycerine and said, with more confidence than she felt, that Tom was on his way.

"I know." He closed his eyes again and thought about Montessori school, where you learned to pour by pouring beans. The beans made a rushing noise, like the ocean—he used to love to pour them back and forth. They went *Wssh wssh* like the waves curling on Stinson Beach where Linda Sanchez lived the night they carried him down the long pink strip of sunset beach. *Wssh wssh.* He smiled—he'd remembered the SorryAss chickens—and slept.

Anne turned back to her book and gobbled the last twenty pages as if someone were going to tear it away from her. She cried for Emily, laughed through her tears at Micawber's colonial success, cried again over Ham's grave, until laughing and crying had all run together like fingerpaint. She closed the book *—how strange, that you could close it just like any other book—* stood and stretched and looked down at her son. He still had his baby-fat cheeks, high round forehead; those cupid-bow lips were still as perfect as a baby doll's—how avidly they had sucked, how desperately in the seconds before the milk had let down. She had talked to him constantly when he was a baby, as if he were a wise being from another planet (which in a sense, she supposed, he was): "This is water." Lying back in the warm bath, sitting him on her still flabby belly. "Funny stuff. Sometimes it's hard . . ." She patty-caked the water with his tiny red hand—perfect baby fingers—and he chortled. "Yeah, funny. And sometimes it's soft . . ." Trickling soft diamond drops over his head. And though he could barely hold his head up he seemed to nod: *Oh yeah, water. Right.*

There was a sound behind her. She turned: Krebs was awake, watching her. He put his finger to his lips, then his ear— *sssh, listen.* A car. Anne climbed the ladder and flopped belly down in the sleeping loft, stretching her neck to see out the low window that ran the width of the loft. "I see . . . no . . . no, gone, no, there . . ." Headlights winking through the mist, through the trees. She gave Krebs the play-by-play. "No, wait, false alarm. That's not the Comet." Then: "Oh shit." It was a BMW. Pierce's BMW. Silver. The ground fog silver in the headlight glow. She couldn't tell how many men were inside.

34

Krebs hurried downstairs to meet Pierce and Tom Straw. Anne heard the men's voices in the Common Room, then the hum of the elevator. She panicked, grabbed her rubber boots from just inside the door and sprinted down the gallery to the spiral staircase before the elevator doors opened on the second floor.

In Dave's kitchen it was dark and clean and smelled like spice and butcher block, bread crumbs and flour, apples and coffee. Anne stood with her back to the swinging door, breathing hard. *Sonofabitch has got me running again,* she thought, stooping to tug her boots on; she made quite sure she *walked* through the pantry and out the side door. It hadn't rained for hours; still the redwoods dripped musically and the grove smelled sweet-sharp and dark green as an herbal shampoo. The paths were only lighted as far as the middle cabins; Anne made a half-hearted foray into the unimaginable blackness beyond and turned back for a flashlight.

Tom was waiting for her on the patio. His navy blue watch-cap and jeans were greenish black in the yellow patio lights. Anne ran to him. He smelled of stale sweat, of damp wool and cigarette smoke, of sixteen hours in the car. It was only when she buried her face against his rough denim that she realized how much she'd missed him, how afraid she must have been. He bent to kiss her. "Whoof," she said. "Burger King breath," and kissed him anyway.

"We stopped in Miller Bay."

She stiffened in his arms. "Did you have a nice drive?" she said furiously. "You boys find enough to talk about?"

Tom let go as if she'd bitten him. *Sure, we scratched and farted and talked about pussy,* he thought sarcastically, but said, "Well yeah, actually: turns out we were both in Nam around the same time."

Well how fucking cozy for you, she thought. "Tom, I didn't want him here. Danny would have been all right."

"All right?" he said incredulously. "What the hell does that mean?" He lowered his voice, conscious of the nearby rooms, of the hospice patients behind the lighted windows overhead. "It's not what *you* wanted. Danny wanted his father."

"You had no right to do what you did without asking me."

"You'd have said no. Anne, the man's his father."

"As far as I'm concerned he's just some jerk who swore he wouldn't come in me." She stopped, dismayed. *God, that sounded ugly. You could say that to a woman and it would only sound like a good bitter joke.* But Tom pivoted on his false leg and turned away. She wanted to say she was sorry, but *he* hadn't. He had pulled off his watchcap and was kneading it in his hands; his hair was stiff with dirt and dried sweat. She crossed the patio after him, splashing through the dark reflective puddles, and had to reach way up on tiptoe to smooth his cowlick. After a moment he relaxed, lowered his head for her like a horse, and she knew they hadn't ruined anything between them. She took his face in both hands and pulled it down to hers.

———

Danny opened his eyes. It was three in the morning; the bedside light was on. He turned his head, which felt so heavy, and saw his father asleep in one sling chair and his mother asleep in the other with the cornflower comforter pulled over her head. Tom Straw snored in the loft.

Pierce opened his eyes, too. "Danny I'm here."

"I know. Tom Straw promised." Danny's eyelids were like waxed paper.

"How do you feel?"

"Okay." Danny's eyes lost focus. What had he needed to say to his father? He struggled to stay awake, but felt like a tv picture that's lost its vertical hold: *flipflipflip.* His father's face floated over him, so close it filled his narrowing field of vision. "See," Danny said after a moment. "My hair grew back." He smelled his father's scent of Camels and Skin Bracer and saw his reflection in the hazel eyes so like his own; the reflection rippled, swelled, distorted as his father's eyes brimmed with tears. His father kissed him on the forehead, the nose, the mouth; Danny tasted the warm tears on his lips.

"Daddy?"

"What?"

"Promise me something?"

"What?"

"Promise first."

Pierce went against every instinct that had ever guided him. It was easy. "I promise."

"Cross your heart?"

"Cross my heart."

"Don't be mad at Mommy anymore."

———

There, thought Danny. He closed his eyes without waiting for a reply. *There.* His father had already promised, after all. His father had crossed his heart. *It would be all right now.* And now the fear of dying was no worse than the fear he used to bring upon himself riding home in the car pool after daycare. He would tell himself: *what if Mommy died? what if burglars came when I was away and killed her? what if the apartment wasn't there, if a stranger opened the door? what if the witches turned her into a witch?* He would dawdle on the way up the walk, up the stairs, until the fear was an almost sexual thrill. Because he *knew* he *knew* he *knew* he would open the door and she would be there and the apartment would smell like her and he would *fly* to her and hug her like they'd been apart for years. And he would feel a thrill because all the fear had been wrong, and there was no more fear anywhere. Until bedtime, anyway. He felt like that now, smelling Skin Bracer, tasting tears, falling asleep.

———

The next morning dawned clear. A bird sang warily as Danny opened his eyes to what seemed like only another dream, a dream of faces, of all the faces floating over him. His father, who'd promised. Tom Straw, who'd kept his promise. Wally's face hovered over him for a long time, round and pale as the man in the moon the night they'd ridden to the saddle ridge east of the sun and west of the moon. Wally started to sing Danny's special song but the tears overcame him. Then his face was gone. The ceiling was high above, white as milk. *Wally don't worry*, thought Danny, *don't cry. I remember: follow the light. I remember.*

Then there was only one last face to see before he closed his eyes. A face he knew better than his own. A face with round cheeks and infinite love and eyes the color of light brown m&m's. His mother bent down to kiss him. *See you later, alligator.*

After awhile, crocodile.

———

Krebs and Wendy left Mr. Mars with his wife and hurried around the gallery to the Mantle Suite. Wally still stood by the intercom just inside the door, snuffling into a blue bandanna. Pierce sat in the chair at the foot of the bed, shoulders hunched forward, hands pressed palms together between his knees. Tom and Anne stood beside the bed, holding hands. With her left hand Anne stroked Danny's head; soft new hair the color of oatmeal ruffled back under her palm.

Wendy threw her arms around Wally as far as they could reach; somehow he shrank into her hug, and she thought of Baby Huey. Krebs stepped up to the bed, looked across Danny's body to Anne. "Shall I pronounce him now?" She looked up from Danny to Krebs, then back, and nodded. How perfect, that he should have asked. How tender his voice had been.

The doctor sat on the edge of the bed and turned back the covers, pulled up Danny's Star Wars pajama top. He placed his stethoscope over Danny's silent heart: in death the child's torso —delicate ribcage, blue white skin, pale nipples round as dimes —was somehow exquisite as a miniature. *This precious human body*, thought Krebs—it was a Buddhist phrase—*this precious human body.* Tom Straw, looking down on the body from his great height, had a different mantra going through his head: *gonna leave this Brokedown Palace . . . this Palace . . . this Brokedown Palace. . . .*

35

Preparing the body always made Wally feel better. He talked to Danny as he pulled on a pair of rubber gloves and snipped the little Foley catheter. "There. Never have to have one of *these* again." It squirted a few cc's of saline and slithered like a red rubber snake into the white enamel basin. "I know you're glad about that." He slipped on a fresh glove—sterile habit—and turned the body over. "Just so we don't have a little accident in the Viewing Room or on the way to Miller Bay." When he was finished he carried the basin to the bathroom, disposed of the contents, washed it out, filled it with warm soapy water, then called to Anne, waiting with Tom out on the gallery, leaning against the railing, not talking, looking down to the Common Room below. Wendy had returned to Mr. Mars in the Skowron Suite; Krebs had taken Pierce for a walk down to the creek.

Danny's feet could scarcely have been cleaner. Still Wally rubbed them with the washcloth while Anne and Tom washed the rest of the body, talking quietly to each other like a couple doing the dishes together after a dinner party. "He was down to skin and bones," Anne observed.

"Pretty soon he'd have just floated away," said Tom, which made Wally smile. Anne washed each hand separately—she noticed as she spread the fingers that they weren't baby hands anymore, but long and sure enough to curve around a pink rubber ball, or hold a fork like a grown-up. He would have been six in late December.

They dressed him in his Dr. Dentons with the trap door and feet. Tom untangled the penguins from the crumpled blankets at the foot of the bed and handed them to Anne, along with Danny's tattered satin-bordered baby blue security blanket. Then Wally carried the body down to the elevator, Anne followed with the blanket and the penguins, and Tom stayed behind to strip the bed.

———

Anne pulled back the top sheet and the cream and crimson Navajo blanket on the Viewing Room bed; Wally set the body down as gently as he would have if Danny had been alive. He cranked up the head of the bed to a twenty-five degree angle while she tucked Danny in. Just going through the old familiar tucking motions overwhelmed Anne for a moment; she did not cry but dropped to her knees and rested her forehead against the rough wool. Felt good. *Please God just numb me out for a while.* Then Tom was beside her. He tried to kneel but the left leg slipped sideways, and he sat down heavily. Anne threw her arms around his neck as if she were drowning. "Tom, I can't do it," she said to his collarbone.

"Can't do what?"

"Can't . . ." She drew back, surprised. "I don't know."

"We'll make it," he said. "The hard part's over. We'll get through it."

———

They did, too. After Pierce and Krebs and the others had in turn said their farewells, Tom wrapped the body in Bea's afghan, and Wally carried it in his arms to the snout-nosed old hospice ambulance, then drove them into Miller Bay. Tom and Anne sat in back with the body, holding hands, not talking much, watching the Bigfoot countryside; the coniferous forest gave way to the hardwoods bright with autumnal madrone, bay, alder and oak, then to the dense coastal brushfields. "Remember on the way up?" said Anne. " 'You can't see 'em. . . .' "

" 'But they're there,' " Tom answered.

Perhaps Anne's prayer for numbness had been answered, for when she sat down with Tom and the funeral director to make the decisions that could no longer be put off, she felt as if she were at a restaurant, and everyone at her table had ordered and the waiter was looking at her with his pad and pencil poised and her mind was a stone blank. Cremation? Bury? Roast beef? Sand dabs? It hardly seemed to matter. Then she thought of simply walking out of there with both hands free, with only Danny's pure memory, and that seemed best. She signed the papers.

It was nearly dark when they returned to the hospice: the silver BMW was gone and Pierce with it. Anne was not sorry to have him gone; in fact, she was reminded of Tom's dumb joke about the Plotnick Diamond: *at least I'm free of the Plotnick Curse, too.* Tom thought it likely that he and Pierce would meet again: his Comet was in the lawyer's garage.

Anne spent the next hour in the kitchen, helping Dave prepare dinner. She was still numb emotionally, but her senses were heightened: the orange yam meat, the sharp green pepper, the fragrant steam from the double boiler, the clean white knife slash in the Santa Claus red radish were real and welcome and *here* and Danny was not.

Tom spent the time before dinner sorting and packing Danny's things. It was a hell of a job. Leah offered to help, but he decided he needed to do it alone. He sat on the floor with Danny's clothes in a heap before him, and began to divide them into two piles: one for Leah's rummage sale, one for the garbage. The little jeans and the red sneakers were as good as new, which seemed terribly wrong to Tom: kid's jeans should have the knees worn through; sneakers should be scuffed holey at the toes and the tongues bent from the kid jamming his feet in and out without untying the laces. The rugby shirt, cords, new bathrobe okay; most of the others too stained. Pajamas worn threadbare: good-bye Star Wars. Dr. Dentons had sailed with Danny. The underwear and the socks were so little: had Danny really been such a peanut?

The toys and books and baseball cards were easier to sort. Most would stay here at the hospice for the next young arrival. The thought angered Tom, and his first tears welled but he blinked them back: not yet: work to do. Besides, what could he hope for—that no child would ever die again? The penguins too would hibernate in the toy chest until needed, except for Pengeena/Shalala. Wally had asked for her; that was all he wanted to remember Danny by.

When the good stuff was all in Safeway paper bags, and all the trash stuffed into an enormous baggie (Tom recalled how once back at the Casa when he had thrown a plastic garbage bag over his shoulder like a sack to carry it down to the garbage, Danny had pointed and laughed and said, "There goes the *bad* Santa with presents for the *bad* kids. Ho ho ho"), Tom found himself sitting on the floor twisting a beat-up old one-size-fits-all Giants cap in his great hands, and crying. He couldn't think what to *do* with it, he'd *tried* to put it with the garbage a half dozen times, but had failed. *It's only cloth and cardboard,* he told himself. *Damn silly thing to crack up over after all this.* But of course it was no more *only* cloth and cardboard than Danny had been *only* flesh and blood: Tom let himself cry for a few minutes, then tossed the black and orange cap into the bottom of his old Navy duffel bag. *Never put off until tomorrow what you can put off until next week.*

But some things couldn't be put off any longer. He picked up the phone to call Frieda. She had loved Danny. She had a right to know.

36

The Gil McDougal was the rustic cabin farthest from the main lodge; it was rarely used for patients even during the summer. Anne swept it out that night after dinner while Tom built a fire. They pushed the twin cots together in front of the stone fireplace, wrapped two bottom sheets sideways over the thin mattresses, and lay on their stomachs watching the flames. Every so often one of them would toss in a handful of redwood needles just for the flash of it, and the fragrance. When the cabin was so warm that the windows had fogged over, Anne took off her shirt and Tom rubbed her back. She didn't talk much, except to say "mmmm" and "there" and "a little higher" and once, as he worked on a particularly troublesome part of her neck, "Joe Miller at the Theosophy lodge says that the head is just a knot tied on the end of your backbone to keep your body from slipping off."

"Is that the same guy who says you can get more stinkin' from thinkin' than from drinkin'?" A thick firelog collapsed in the middle with an almost human groan.

"Mmmm-hmmm." Anne's sore spine and ribs, neck and shoulders and sacrum, welcomed the manipulation of his powerful hands—she had been so tense for so long that her body felt like one of those Invisible Woman models, with a hard plastic snap-together skeleton. Anne sighed and closed her eyes.

———

The cotsprings squeaked when Tom got up to throw another log on the fire. Anne opened her eyes. "Was I asleep?"

"Only for an hour." He pulled off his boots, jeans, and leg and climbed into bed in his T-shirt. She rolled toward him, over the great divide onto his mattress, and said, "I'm going to roll a joint. Want some?"

"They say it deadens the feelings."

"A big one, then."

——

He smoked with her, and they made love. It wasn't the best in the world, but it wasn't the worst either: the fire crackled and the metal cot squeaked and for the first time in recent history they each got to moan and groan and *oh baby!* as loudly as they wanted to. They even overplayed that part of it a little, but it was fun.

——

Anne awoke at one, Tom a few minutes later. "I tried to cry but I couldn't," she said. It was black dark.

"It'll come."

"I'm scared, waiting."

He took her hands in his and brought her fingertips to his face so she could read his smile like a blind woman. "Joe the prospector," he said, "it's me, Moe. What else can go wrong?"

"No fair, no dumb jokes."

"Baby, it's all over now. We *made* it. *Danny* made it. And you'll cry when you're goddam good and ready."

——

Three o'clock. "Tom?"

He looked up from his book. "What?"

"I couldn't sleep."

"You better look under the bed then, 'cause *somebody* was sure snoring in here."

"Tell me about Maui again," she murmured, like: *tell me about da rabbits again, George.*

"Okay. This time next week . . ." He shifted, stretched his arm out; she snuggled in. "Picture a black sand beach. Strawberry daquiris on the lanai. Fish that taste like buttered chicken. *White* sand beaches. Sleeping late. There's a volcano where you'd *swear* you were on another planet. Magic mushrooms. Onions sweet as apples. *Red* sand beaches. Snorkeling. Fish God had to invent new colors for. *Piña coladas* on the lanai."

"And nobody dies," said Anne.

"Absolutely not. Nobody dies on Maui."

"Promise?"

"Cross my heart."

——

Krebs conducted a brief service in the Common Room the following evening after dinner. He stood facing the others with his back to the fire, as always, and cleared his throat. "Just when I'm beginning to think that I'm starting to figure it all out," he began, "why people die, or why there's suffering . . . when it's like a jigsaw puzzle that's put together just enough so you can pretty much tell what it's going to look like. . . . It's as if for me there's always one key piece missing, and that piece has to do with kids. If I could only figure out the answer to why kids like Danny have to suffer and die, I'd know what this—(he spread his hands)—this *creation* is all about." He paused—he appeared to be searching for the right words, but in fact this was the only part of the speech where he knew exactly what he was going to say. He said it directly to Anne, on the couch. "I still don't know what the answer to the question is, but after knowing Danny for three months I'm more certain than I ever was that there *is* an answer." He stopped. "That's all *I* have to say. I think Wally's got a song for us."

Wally stepped up beside him and tuned the guitar with his back to the others. When he turned to face them he said, "I know what song Danny would have wanted me to sing, but I don't know if Anne wants to hear." She waved him on grandly, and he smiled and sang *Danny Boy*. All four verses. And yes, Anne was crying by the end, but it was not so much the song as it was the sight of that silly stuffed penguin peeking out from Wally's breast pocket that had freed her tears. She buried her face against Tom Straw's shoulder and wept for herself and her son and everybody else who believed—who *had* to believe—that there *was* an answer, in the face of what was, after all, very little physical evidence.